"Throw
it away?
…I would
never
do such
a cruel
thing. I'll
treasure
it."

"...No, well, um...if it's all right, I guess I'll have some, but, uh..."

Amane felt an innocence in her, and her pure smile was beautiful enough to take his breath away. She was really exceptionally cute.

The
Angel
Next Door
Spoils Me
Rotten

Saekisan

ILLUSTRATION BY
Hanekoto

"...This is exactly why you must tidy up, because otherwise things like this are bound to happen."

The instant a small "Ah!" escaped Mahiru's mouth, Amane dived across the room, aiming for the spot where he thought Mahiru would most likely fall.

A light, sweet fragrance mixed with the musty smell of the dust that had been kicked up in the panic.

"You
don't
want
any?"

Contents

Amane Fujimiya

A first-year high school student who began living alone at the start of the semester. He is poor at every type of housework and leads a self-indulgent life. He has few friends and tends to put himself down.

Mahiru Shiina

A classmate who lives next door to Amane. She is the most beautiful girl in school. She's well-behaved, gets great grades, always wears a smile, and is called an angel by her peers.

©Hanekoto

The Angel Next Door Spoils Me Rotten

1

Saekisan

ILLUSTRATION BY
Hanekoto

YEN
ON

NEW YORK

The Angel Next Door Spoils Me Rotten 1

Saekisan

TRANSLATION BY NICOLE WILDER ✳ COVER ART BY HANEKOTO

OTONARI NO TENSHISAMA NI ITSUNOMANIKA DAMENINGEN NI SARETEITA KEN Vol. 1
Copyright © 2019 Saekisan
Cover Illustration © 2019 Hanekoto
All rights reserved.
Original Japanese edition published in 2019 by SB Creative Corp.
This English edition is published by arrangement with SB Creative Corp., Tokyo in care of Tuttle-Mori Agency, Inc., Tokyo.

English translation © 2020 by Yen Press, LLC

Yen On
150 West 30th Street, 19th Floor
New York, NY 10001

Visit us at yenpress.com ✳ facebook.com/yenpress ✳ twitter.com/yenpress
yenpress.tumblr.com ✳ instagram.com/yenpress

First Yen On Edition: December 2020

Yen On is an imprint of Yen Press, LLC.
The Yen On name and logo are trademarks of Yen Press, LLC.

Library of Congress Cataloging-in-Publication Data
Names: Saekisan, author. | Hanekoto, illustrator. | Wilder, Nicole, translator.
Title: The angel next door spoils me rotten / Saekisan ; illustration by Hanekoto ; translation by Nicole Wilder.
Other titles: Otonari no tenshi-sama ni Itsu no ma ni ka dame ningen ni sareteita ken. English
Description: First Yen On edition. | New York : Yen On, 2020–
Identifiers: LCCN 2020043583 | ISBN 9781975319236 (v. 1 ; trade paperback)
Subjects: CYAC: Love—Fiction.
Classification: LCC PZ7.1.S2413 An 2020 | DDC [Fic]—dc23
LC record available at https://lccn.loc.gov/2020043583

ISBNs: 978-1-9753-1923-6 (paperback)
978-1-9753-1924-3 (ebook)

5 7 9 10 8 6 4

TPA

Printed in South Korea

Chapter 1

Meeting an Angel

"...What're you doing?"

The first time Amane Fujimiya spoke to Mahiru Shiina was when he caught sight of her sitting on a swing in the park, in the middle of the pouring rain.

This was Amane's first year as a high school student. He'd recently begun living alone in a nearby apartment building. Little did he know when he first moved in that his next-door neighbor was a veritable angel on Earth.

Of course, calling her an angel was just a figure of speech, but Mahiru Shiina was such a beautiful, sweet girl that the comparison seemed entirely fitting.

Her straight, well-groomed, flaxen hair was always silky smooth and lustrous. The girl's pale, milky-white skin was always soft, as if it had never been anything less than perfect. From her shapely nose and large eyes rimmed with long eyelashes to her delicate, dewy pink lips, every part of her looked like it had been sculpted by the practiced hand of a true master.

Amane went to the same high school as Mahiru and was in the same grade, so he'd heard plenty about her. Mostly, people talked about her beauty or how she was accomplished in both academics and sports.

As it happened, Mahiru always got the top score on exams and was a real ace in gym class, too. Amane was in a different class, so he didn't know all the details, but if the rumors were anything to judge by, Mahiru was some kind of superhuman being.

Truly, she seemed without a flaw—attractive in face and figure and an excellent student. Perhaps most surprising was that she wasn't the least bit stuck-up about it. With her quiet, modest personality, it was no wonder she was so popular.

Living next door to such a beautiful girl would've gotten most boys practically salivating at the mere thought. Amane, however, didn't intend to make a fuss over her or try to get too close.

He certainly wouldn't deny that Mahiru Shiina was beautiful, but she had never been more than a neighbor to him. There hadn't really been any opportunities for them to talk, and not once did he consider approaching her himself.

If they did somehow become involved in some fashion, it would definitely make a lot of other boys jealous, and that'd be trouble. Amane knew it was better to remain amicable next-door neighbors and avoid the wrath of her other admirers.

It was possible to appreciate a charming girl without falling in love with her, after all. Amane recognized that Mahiru was the kind of girl best cherished from afar and had contented himself with existing in her life as only her neighbor.

Thus, when Amane caught sight of her looking lost in thought and alone in the pouring rain without an umbrella, he couldn't help but stop and stare, wondering what she might be doing.

The downpour was heavy enough to send most everyone else scurrying home, but there she was, sitting all by herself on a swing in the park between their school and their apartment building.

What is she doing in the rain? Amane wondered.

Everything was gloomy beneath the darkened sky, and the rain, relentless since that morning, only made it even more difficult to see. Mahiru's conspicuous flaxen hair and her school uniform made it impossible to miss her, however, even veiled by the dismal weather.

Amane did not know why she was sitting there without an umbrella, letting herself get soaked. Mahiru didn't appear to be waiting for someone, nor did she seem at all concerned by the rain. As far as Amane could tell, Mahiru was simply staring off into the distance.

Her face was tilted slightly upward, and though she was always pale, her complexion appeared downright pallid. If she wasn't careful, she was sure to catch a cold, but even so, Mahiru sat there quietly, not making any move to head home.

If she's content to sit there, it probably isn't my place to interfere, Amane thought as he made his way quickly past the park. He took one last look and could see that Mahiru's face was screwed up as if she might cry.

Amane scratched his head nervously. He wasn't really looking to make any kind of connection with her or anything, but it seemed wrong to him to ignore another person who was making such a pained expression.

"…What're you doing?"

When he called out to her in the bluntest voice possible, trying to convey that he was not a threat, she tossed her long hair, now heavy with water, and looked at him.

Mahiru's face was as lovely as ever.

Even wet with rain, its radiance was not dulled. In fact, every droplet only seemed to enhance her elegant features. One could say she was dripping with beauty.   ·

She stared at him with large, striking eyes.

Mahiru must have been vaguely aware of Amane as her next-door neighbor because they occasionally passed each other in the morning. However, the look in her caramel-colored eyes revealed that she was slightly guarded—someone she had never really spoken with had suddenly called out to her.

"Fujimiya? May I help you?"

Amane was rather shocked that Mahiru had remembered his name, but at the same time, he also figured that this level of familiarity most likely wouldn't cause her to drop her guard. It was only to be expected that Mahiru would raise her defenses when confronted by a stranger, even if he wasn't entirely unknown.

She probably didn't want much to do with the opposite sex. It certainly seemed like she received plenty of romantic advances from the boys at school, regardless of what year they were in. Would anyone have blamed Mahiru for suspecting Amane of harboring an ulterior motive?

"I don't really need anything. I was just wondering why you were sitting in a place like this, all alone in the rain."

"Oh, you were? I'm grateful for your concern, but I'm here simply because I want to be. Don't worry about me."

There was no edge of suspicion in Mahiru's soft, listless voice, but it was also clear that she had no intention of opening up to Amane.

All right, suit yourself.

It was clear that there was something going on with her, but she didn't seem to want Amane to get involved, and he wasn't particularly inclined to pursue the matter any further.

Amane had only approached her on a whim. He'd simply been curious about her situation; that was all. It wasn't really his concern. If this was what she wanted to be doing, then that was just fine by him.

Amane sensed the evanescent beauty regarding him with some

suspicion. He was sure that Mahiru was wondering why he'd even bothered speaking to her at all.

"Ah, I see," he offered in reply.

Pressing the issue wouldn't get him anywhere, so Amane decided to withdraw. There was no shared history between them, and perhaps that was for the best. The decision to leave her alone was an easy one.

Even with a very good reason to depart, Amane still didn't think it seemed right to abandon her—and thoroughly soaked to boot.

"You'll catch a cold, so take this and go home. No need to bother giving it back."

Deciding this would be the one and only time he meddled, Amane offered Mahiru his own umbrella. After all, he didn't want her to get sick or anything.

Amane handed over the umbrella—or to put it more accurately, he gave her little choice but to accept. Without giving Mahiru a chance to reply, he turned away and took off. As he left the scene, Amane heard Mahiru calling to him.

Whatever she was trying to say was too quiet and became drowned out by the rain. Amane didn't stop or turn around until the park was well behind him.

He had cared enough about the girl possibly catching a cold to foist his umbrella on her, so he didn't feel that guilty about the fact that he had originally intended to ignore her altogether.

At any rate, Mahiru had refused his attempt to start a conversation, and Amane didn't intend to get any closer to her, either. After all, they had no connection to each other beyond this.

Amane assured himself along those lines as he made his way home.

Chapter 2

A Cold — and Being Nursed by an Angel

"Amane, your sniffling's annoying."

"*You're* annoying."

The next day, it was Amane who'd ended up with the cold.

As his classmate and good friend Itsuki Akazawa had pointed out, Amane had been trying and failing to snort everything back up his nose. Trying to exhale only resulted in a terrible, wet, burbling sound.

Amane wasn't sure whether it was because his nose was stuffed up or as a result of the cold itself, but a throbbing pain was spreading across the back of his head. He had taken some over-the-counter medicine, but it wasn't making a dent in his symptoms at all. Truly, Amane was a sad sight. His congested face twisted in nasal distress as he became well acquainted with a tissue.

Itsuki looked at him, not with concern but exasperation.

"You were just fine yesterday, dude."

"I got caught in the rain."

"Aw, chin up. Wait, didn't you have an umbrella yesterday?"

"…I gave it to someone."

Naturally, there was no way that Amane could openly admit at school that he'd given it to Mahiru, so he kept things vague.

Incidentally, he'd caught a glimpse of Mahiru earlier that day. She'd looked rather well, not ill at all. Amane couldn't help but laugh. Things had gotten completely flipped around. It was his own fault—he'd neglected to warm up in the bath when he'd gotten home.

"Don'cha think you were being a little too nice, lending out your umbrella when it was pouring like that?"

"Not really. Even if I did, no point complaining about it now."

"And who did you give it to anyway? Who was worth catching a cold?"

"...A, uh, a lost little kid?"

Can't really call her a kid with that body, though... Well, that and the fact that we're the same age. Although, her face did look kinda lost...

Something clicked when Amane thought of the unusual encounter that way. Her expression had been exactly that of a lost little kid searching for their parent.

"Well, what a kind and upstanding gentleman you are!" Itsuki laughed, unaware of the feelings bubbling up in Amane's chest as he recalled his meeting with Mahiru the day before. "But you know, even if you let someone borrow your umbrella or whatever, I bet your real problem was that you got lazy and didn't warm up afterward. That's why you're dying."

"...How do you know that?" Amane shot back.

"Well, you don't exactly take good care of yourself. That much was obvious the moment I saw your place. That's why you got sick, dumbass."

Amane couldn't really argue with Itsuki's friendly ribbing. It was true that he didn't have the most wholesome lifestyle. To elaborate, he was bad at keeping things tidy, and his room was always a total mess. What's more, he subsisted on a diet of convenience-store meals and nutritional supplements. The only time he had a decent meal was when he went out to eat once in a blue moon. Itsuki often grew frustrated with him, asking him how he could live like that.

Knowing his friend kept such habits, Itsuki was not at all surprised that Amane had caught a cold overnight.

"You oughtta go straight home today and rest up. Tomorrow's Saturday, so focus on getting better," Itsuki advised.

"I will…," Amane replied.

"If only you had a nice girl to nurse you back to health like I do." Itsuki's lips curled up at his slight boast.

"Shut up. I don't need to hear that from a guy who's already got a girlfriend." Amane slapped away the box of tissues in front of him with the back of his hand, intensely irritated.

As the day wore on, Amane's condition continued to deteriorate.

The headache and runny nose were soon accompanied by throat pain and a fatigue that permeated his body. Though he single-mindedly hurried home after school, his body seemed to be losing its battle against the disease, and his pace was agonizingly slow.

Eventually, he reached the lobby of his apartment building and forced his heavy legs to move him into the elevator, where he leaned against the wall. His breathing was rougher than usual, and he felt hot.

Somehow, Amane had been able to endure it while he was at school, but he'd let his guard down now that home was in sight, and his condition had suddenly taken a turn for the worse. Even the peculiar floating sensation of riding in the elevator, normally not a concern, was now a source of dull agony.

When the elevator eventually stopped on Amane's floor, he staggered out on leaden feet and began to shuffle toward his apartment. Almost immediately, he was confronted by a sight that caused him to seize up, however.

Right there in front of him was the girl he had not expected to speak to again, her shimmery flaxen hair fluttering in the breeze. Her lovely features were full of life, her complexion vibrant and glowing.

Even though she had definitely seemed the more likely candidate to catch a cold, she was healthy as could be. The benefits of her self-care were on vivid display.

In her hands, Mahiru was gripping the umbrella that Amane had forced on her the day before, neatly folded and closed.

She must have come to return it, even though I told her she didn't have to, Amane reasoned.

"...Really, you don't need to give it back," he said aloud.

"It's only natural to return something you borrowed..." Mahiru hesitated as soon as she got a good look at Amane's face. "Um. You have a fever, don't you...?"

"...It's got nothing to do with you."

Amane frowned. This was perhaps the worst possible time to run into Mahiru—and all over a stupid umbrella, too. It was the kind of thing that shouldn't have been worth the trouble of returning. Mahiru was smart, however, and was sure to quickly figure out how Amane had caught a cold.

"But you only became sick because you loaned me your umbrella..."

"That's totally unrelated. Besides, I loaned it to you on a whim."

"It most certainly is related! The fact is that you caught a cold because I was out there in the rain."

"I said it's fine, really. It's not something you need to worry about."

From Amane's perspective, he had done her the favor for his own self-satisfaction, and he didn't want her fussing over him now.

However, Mahiru didn't seem likely to just leave him be. Anxiety was written across her graceful features.

"...So yeah, it's all good. See ya." Their back-and-forth was quickly growing taxing, so Amane decided to force his way out from under Mahiru's questioning and concern.

Swaying and staggering, he snatched the umbrella from her and pulled his keys out of his pocket. Everything was going fine, so far. Unfortunately, Amane fumbled quite a bit as he opened the door to his apartment. The moment he got it open, all the strength left his body.

Perhaps the feeling of relief on finally entering his home was to blame for how his body unexpectedly keeled over toward the railing behind him.

Although Amane was alarmed, he trusted that the railing was solid enough that it wouldn't break, and he wouldn't fall. Surely it would catch him, and he'd be fine.

The impact will probably hurt a bit, but I guess there's no avoiding it…, Amane thought, resigning himself to the pain.

However, someone firmly took hold of his arm and hauled him back upright.

"…Just as I thought; I can't leave you alone like this." Amane heard a fragile voice through his feverish haze. "I'll repay your favor."

Amane's head swam as he tried to make sense of the words, but he quickly gave up. Before he understood what was happening, Mahiru had propped up his limp body and opened the door to his apartment.

"I'm going to help you inside. There's no other way, so please forgive the intrusion."

Her tone of voice was quiet but left no room for argument.

The fever-stricken Amane had no willpower to resist. He was pulled along, entering his apartment with a girl his own age for the first time in his life. It was true that he didn't have a girlfriend to nurse him back to health, but it seemed that an angel had descended to care for him instead.

Thoroughly addled with fever, Amane had forgotten all about the sorry state of his place until it was too late. It wasn't until he saw the condition his home was in that he regretted ever letting Mahiru enter.

His apartment was spacious. It even had a spare room in addition to the bedroom and main living space.

It was quite an extravagant dwelling for a person living alone, but Amane's parents were fairly well-off and had decided on this place after considering the safety of the neighborhood and the convenience of nearby transportation. Amane had always thought that spending so much money on housing was unnecessary. The apartment was much too large for a single person anyway. Still, his parents had insisted, and he wasn't about to complain.

Setting that aside, Amane did live alone, and he was a typical teenage boy. Things were not kept especially tidy. Various items were scattered all over the living room, and needless to say, there was the state of the bedroom.

"This is too pitiful to look at." The angel, Amane's savior, gave him a frank assessment of his living conditions. Such harshness was quite the contrast to her charming appearance.

Amane could hardly argue—it really was a sorry sight. If he'd known that he'd be bringing a stranger into his home, he might have moved some things, perhaps tidied up a bit, but it was too late for that now.

Mahiru let a sigh slip from her glossy lips, but undeterred, she set to moving Amane into his bedroom. They nearly tripped along the way, and Amane vowed to do some serious cleaning sometime soon.

"First, I'm going out for a moment, so please go ahead and change clothes before I get back. You can do that, right?" Mahiru asked.

"...You're coming back?"

"My conscience would never let me rest if I left you alone like this, even to sleep," Mahiru responded bluntly, apparently feeling the same way now that Amane had felt toward her when she was soaking wet the day before.

Amane did not argue any further. After Mahiru left the room, he obediently did as he was told and started changing out of his school uniform.

"It's really a mess in here; there's nowhere to even step… How can anyone live like this…?"

As he was changing, Amane heard an exasperated voice, quietly coming from the next room, and felt quite ashamed.

After changing clothes, he went to lie down and must have fallen asleep without realizing it, because when he managed to lift his heavy eyelids again, flaxen hair was the first thing he saw.

Following the hair, Amane looked up to see Mahiru standing silently at his side, peering down at him. The whole scene felt like something out of a dream.

"…What time is it?" Amane asked, confused.

"Seven in the evening," Mahiru answered matter-of-factly. "You slept for several hours."

As Amane propped himself up, Mahiru handed him some sports drink that she had poured into a cup. He accepted it gratefully and brought it to his lips, then finally was able to take a look at his surroundings.

Maybe it was because he had slept, but he felt just a little bit better than before.

He realized that his head felt cool and pressed a hand to his forehead. When he did, his fingers registered a slightly starchy sensation, like cloth.

There was a cooling sheet stuck to him. Amane was sure he didn't have any of those at his place, and he looked up at Mahiru.

"I brought it from home," she answered immediately.

Amane had no cooling sheets in his apartment—and no sports drinks, either. Mahiru must have brought that over as well.

"…Thank you. Sorry for all the trouble."

"It's fine."

There was nothing Amane could do but smile bitterly at Mahiru's curt answer.

Mahiru had only offered to play nurse because she felt guilty. It definitely didn't mean that she genuinely wanted to spend time with Amane. He was sure of that. She was already talking with a boy she barely knew—and alone in his apartment no less. That she would make sure there were no misunderstandings about how she felt was only natural.

"For the time being, I brought you the medicine that was on top of your desk. It's better to take it with something in your stomach… Are you hungry at all?" Mahiru asked gently.

"Mm, a little bit," Amane answered.

"Oh really? Well, in that case, I made some rice porridge, so you're welcome to have some."

"…Huh, you made it yourself?"

"Is there anyone else here but me? If you don't want it, I'll eat it all alone."

"No, I'll eat it! Please let me eat it!"

Amane had never imagined Mahiru preparing a homemade meal for him. For a moment, he was caught off guard.

Frankly, he had no idea whether Mahiru even knew how to cook, but he'd never heard rumors of her failing cooking class, so he was fairly confident it wouldn't be awful.

Although Mahiru looked surprised at Amane's sudden bow and insistence that he would eat her food, she nodded before handing him the thermometer that was sitting on the side table.

"I'll bring it to you, so take your temperature first."

"Okay," Amane said, taking the thermometer out of its sleeve. He began unbuttoning his shirt, and Mahiru quickly turned away.

"Do it after I leave the room, please." There was a slight rise in her voice, and Amane spied that the girl's pale cheeks were tinged red.

Amane hadn't thought twice about taking off his shirt in front of her. He didn't consider it anything to worry about, but Mahiru was clearly flustered. Perhaps she wasn't accustomed to seeing much skin.

Mahiru's alabaster cheeks were faintly rosy, and she kept her blushing face turned away, trembling. Even the tips of her ears appeared to be changing hue, making her shyness almost palpable.

…Ah, I think I kind of understand why all the other boys are always saying how cute she is.

Amane had never denied that Mahiru was very pretty, but he'd also never had any special feelings for her beyond a commonplace appreciation for her gentle beauty. He had looked at her like something akin to a work of art and had been content to admire her like one would a distant masterpiece.

Mahiru wasn't some far-off thing anymore, though. She was in his apartment, looking slightly flustered and very shy. In that moment, Amane saw her as a girl and not some idol, and it was strangely adorable.

The two didn't have the kind of relationship where Amane could just up and say that he thought Mahiru looked cute, however. It would probably just come across as weird if he tried, which was why he kept his impressions to himself.

"…Well then, do you think you could go get the rice porridge?" he asked.

"Y-you don't have to tell me," Mahiru answered dismissively. "I'll be right back." She turned and made a swift exit, her footsteps pattering away.

It took Mahiru some time to leave, maybe because she was trembling or maybe because of all the clutter. Probably the latter.

After vacantly watching her go, Amane wondered again how things had turned out this way and let out a soft breath that was not quite a sigh.

…Well, I guess she just feels guilty over what happened.

Normally, it would be unthinkable to follow a stranger into his apartment. It was too dangerous; she could be attacked or something.

Mahiru taking such a chance on Amane must've meant she was worried about him. Maybe his apparent lack of interest helped put her at ease. Either way, Amane didn't think it mattered. He was certain Mahiru was only helping him out of a sense of obligation.

Amane's mind, still slightly delirious with fever, continued to wander as he waited. Then came a hesitant knock at the door.

"…I've brought the porridge."

At the sound of Mahiru's concerned voice from the next room, Amane remembered again that he had loosened his clothing in order to take his temperature.

"I haven't taken my temperature yet," he called back.

"I thought I told you to take it while I was out of the room, though…"

"Sorry, I spaced out."

Amane apologized meekly and stuck the thermometer in his armpit. After a few moments, it let out a muffled electronic beep. When he yanked it out and held it up to look at the screen, it showed a temperature of 38.3 degrees Celsius. It wasn't bad enough to go to the hospital, but it was still pretty high.

"Okay, I'm finished," Amane said as he put his shirt back on.

Mahiru entered with obvious aprehension, carrying a tray with a lidded bowl resting on it. She looked relieved, probably because Amane had fixed his clothes.

"What was your temperature?" she asked.

"Thirty-eight point three. I'll be better after I take some medicine and get some more sleep."

"…Over-the-counter medicine only treats the symptoms and

won't eliminate the virus itself, you know. You need to rest properly and let your immune system do its job."

Such harsh scolding, even if it was coming from a place of concern, embarrassed Amane.

Mahiru sighed in exasperation and placed the tray and bowl on the side table, then opened the lid. Inside was rice porridge with pickled plums. It looked severely watered down—maybe 70 percent porridge to 30 percent water. Perhaps Mahiru had done that intentionally because she'd thought it'd be easier on Amane's stomach. She'd likely added the plums because of their reputation as being good for fighting colds.

The dish wasn't steaming, but it gave off a faint warmth. Amane guessed that Mahiru hadn't brought it straight from the stove but had instead made sure to let it to cool down first.

Ignoring Amane as he stared at the porridge, Mahiru ladled some into a smaller bowl with a clearly practiced hand. She had broken the pickled fruit up a bit for him and had apparently even neatly removed the pits. The red of the plums and the white of the rice mixed easily.

"Here you go. It shouldn't be too hot."

"Mm, thank you."

Mahiru gave Amane a puzzled look as he received the bowl, but then he merely stared at the porridge while his spoon hovered over it.

"…What is it; you want me to feed you? Sorry, but that's not on the menu," Mahiru asserted.

"Nobody asked for that, okay? It's just… So I guess you can cook, too, huh?" Amane asked.

"I live alone, so of course I can." The girl's words stung, a heavy reminder of Amane's own domestic failures. "But before you learn to cook, you should learn to clean up your room, Fujimiya."

"Yes, ma'am…"

Mahiru had quickly and thoroughly put him in his place. Amane grumbled quietly and scooped up some of the porridge, stuffing the spoon into his mouth in a bid to end the conversation.

The flavor of the lightly salted rice spread across his tongue as he ate the porridge. The mellow sourness of the pickled plums pulled it all together. It was truly a dish with a perfect balance of flavors.

Amane didn't like pickled plums that were too salty, but these had a milder taste and a bit of sweetness. They were actually a favorite of his. Often, he liked to top green tea rice with pickled plums.

"It's good."

"Thanks for saying so. Though, really, once you've tasted one rice porridge, I think you've probably tasted them all." Mahiru's answer appeared indifferent, save for the very slightest beginnings of a smile.

Without meaning to, Amane found himself staring at the beautiful girl's relieved expression. Something about it seemed quite different from the more outgoing smile he occasionally caught her wearing at school.

"…Fujimiya?" Mahiru asked.

"Sorry, it's nothing," he answered.

Amane thought it a shame that such a beautiful smile had been so fleeting, though he kept the musing to himself. Instead, he shoveled spoonful after spoonful of porridge into his mouth.

"…Anyhow, you rest today. And make sure to replenish your fluids. If you need to wipe away sweat, use this. I've put water into your washbowl, so make sure to wet it and wring it out before wiping, okay?"

After Amane had eaten, Mahiru diligently prepared an unopened sports drink, readied the bowl of water, and laid out a towel and spare cooling sheets. All had been carefully placed on the side table in Amane's bedroom.

There was no way Mahiru was going to stay over at the home of a boy she barely knew. Amane wouldn't have stood for it if she'd tried. Thus, Mahiru had prepared everything Amane could've needed while he rested, and he was grateful for her diligence, though he stared at her the whole time she got everything ready.

This is an awful lot just to repay a favor. Once this is over, I guess we won't have much reason to interact. It's a one-off thing, a freak occurrence; that's all.

Well, since we won't be talking ever again, I guess it's all right to ask about that thing I want to know.

Whether from the medicine or his nap, Amane's head felt clearer, though he was still exhausted.

"Hey, there's something I've been wondering…," he started.

"What is it?" Mahiru turned to look at him from where she was setting up all the essentials he'd need.

"Why were you sitting out in the rain? Did you have a fight with your boyfriend or something?" The strange behavior that'd kicked off this whole chain of events had been on Amane's mind since he'd first noticed it. Mahiru had been rocking back and forth on a swing in the pouring rain. What could she have been doing there?

It was precisely because Amane had been curious about Mahiru's slight resemblance to a lost child that he'd offered her his umbrella in the first place. He'd never discovered why she'd been out there in the storm to begin with, however.

Amane had thought Mahiru had been waiting for someone, so he'd guessed that there was a boy she was dating, even wondering if perhaps she and her boyfriend had gotten into an argument. In response to Amane's question, Mahiru looked at him as if she was fed up.

"Sorry, but I don't have a boyfriend, and I have no plans to get one," she replied.

"Huh? Why?" Amane asked almost unconsciously.

"Let me ask you, why did you assume I was dating someone?"

"With how popular you are, I thought you'd have at least one or two boyfriends."

Something about this back-and-forth made Mahiru seem much more like a normal girl to Amane. She was kind but strong-willed. To other people, though, he was sure she seemed quite different. Mahiru was a beautiful girl who was tidy, sweet, quiet, and humble. Her pretty face, so lovely that she was often called an angel, turned heads wherever she went, and her body was petite but possessed abundant curves. The briefest sight of her instilled a strange, momentary feeling of wanting to protect her. That quality, combined with her excellent sense of style, made her an object of desire for many a schoolboy.

On top of all that, her grades kept her at the top of her class, and she was an all-around excellent athlete. What's more, Amane had just learned firsthand that she was good at cooking, too. That certainly wouldn't hurt her popularity.

Just one glance was enough to know there must have been plenty of guys who were after her, and Amane knew for a fact that quite a few of his own classmates had romantic feelings for Mahiru. She could've had her pick of the litter, and it hadn't occurred to him that she might not be seeing anyone.

That was what Amane had meant when he'd said that thing about one or two boyfriends, but the moment she'd heard those words, Mahiru's expression had stiffened, if only for a moment.

"I don't have a boyfriend, and what's more, I'm not the kind of girl who would keep the company of several boys at once. It's absolutely out of the question."

Mahiru's eyes were so cold, they sent a shiver down Amane's spine. He realized immediately that he'd stepped on some kind of social land mine.

It might have been because of his sickness, but he felt a chill pass over him, and the room seemed drafty all of a sudden.

"Sorry, that's not what I meant. I apologize," Amane said.

"...No, I'm sorry for getting fired up."

Mahiru bowing her head seemed to disperse the cold, tense atmosphere of the room. More than being "fired up," Mahiru's icy reply to Amane's question had been like a blizzard, though he knew better than to point that out.

"Anyway, that's not what was going on at all. I was just trying to cool my head a bit... And I really am sorry that you caught a cold because you were worried about me," Mahiru explained.

"It's fine. I mean, it was my decision, after all. I feel kind of guilty about all this, actually. I only gave you the umbrella as a spur-of-the-moment kind of thing. I'll try not to bother you once this is all over."

Amane was sure that Mahiru was only there to help out of some sense of obligation, but when she heard what he had to say, she blinked a few times and gave him a curious look. It must have intrigued her to hear that he wouldn't be troubling her again.

"We don't really have any reason to interact, so it's not like it'll be a big deal. I mean, even if you're the most beautiful girl in our grade, and a genius, and everyone calls you an angel, I wasn't trying to hook up with you; I swear. You don't think that this was some kind of scheme or something, do you?" Amane inquired.

Mahiru looked away a little awkwardly. A bitter smile spread across her lips, as if she'd been waiting for Amane to say those exact words. Finally, he realized that she wasn't just acting cagey. Mahiru had probably wound up in that sort of situation a few times before. A guy trying to get in with a beautiful girl by making her feel indebted was, unfortunately, not unheard of.

It explained why Mahiru had been so wary of Amane that day in the rain. She hadn't been upset at him; she'd just been trying to protect herself.

"It must be so irritating. Being bothered by guys you don't even like," Amane said.

"Well, that's true, but..." Mahiru's voice trailed off.

"Called it," quipped Amane, a little surprised to hear her admit it.

So the quiet, charming, model student, the one everybody makes a big fuss over, the one everybody calls an angel, does have things she doesn't like. Why, she even gets annoyed from time to time, just like the rest of us mortals. The thought gave Amane the sudden impression that he was seeing the real Mahiru for the first time.

Unfortunately, the way she glared back at Amane seemed to suggest that she was really regretting having ever met him. It looked like she resented him for making her reveal how she really felt.

Further proof that the angelic honor student has real emotions hidden deep down, Amane thought.

"I don't really see the problem with that," admitted Amane. "Actually, I'm relieved. It's nice to hear that the angel finds that stuff just as annoying as normal humans."

"...Please stop calling me that." Mahiru obviously hated the title others had given her. With disapproval in her eyes, she continued to gaze at Amane.

Even her displeasure seemed interesting to Amane, who smiled again and said, "Not to worry, I won't bother you again without a good reason."

Mahiru's eyes opened wide as if his declaration had caught her by surprise. With the faintest whisper of a smile crossing her lips, she bowed sharply and left.

Amane lay in bed, staring vacantly up at the ceiling while thinking about Mahiru.

Even though the medicine had taken effect, he was, unsurprisingly, still feeling sluggish. If he relaxed, sleep would surely claim him in no time at all. He closed his eyes and reflected on the events of the day.

No one would ever believe him if he told them that he'd been nursed back to health by an angel with a surprisingly sharp tongue. The day's events were a secret shared only by Amane and Mahiru.

It feels kinda weird to call it a secret. It's more like it'd be a real pain to explain the whole story. It's just easier not to tell anybody, that's all, Amane reasoned.

As he slowly lost consciousness, Amane told himself that, when tomorrow came, he and Mahiru would be nothing more than mere acquaintances again.

Chapter 3

The Angel's Generosity

As Amane had anticipated, he and Mahiru had returned to being nothing more than two people who attended the same school.

He'd been feeling much better the following day and had happened to run into Mahiru when he went out to shop at the convenience store, but they hadn't said very much to each other. Amane did catch that Mahiru looked a little relieved to see him well on his way to recovery.

Nothing changed back at school on the following Monday, either. The two were back to being strangers. The only tiny difference was that now, whenever they encountered each other on the way to school, she would greet him with a quick bow. That was all.

"Oh, Amane, you feeling better?"

"I'm good, thanks."

It seemed that Itsuki had also been worried about Amane. He'd been in rather bad shape last Friday, after all. Amane's condition had been the first thing Itsuki asked about when they saw each other outside the school building. Itsuki had even sent Amane a text over the weekend: *"You're not dead, right?"*

Amane had sent back a message that he was fine, but it seemed Itsuki had only been half-convinced, because he let out a deep sigh of relief when he saw in person how much better his friend was feeling.

"Yeah, well, when I saw you in such bad shape, even I started to worry, man! It's all good if you're better now. You oughtta take better care of yourself. Start by cleaning your room or somethin'."

"You sound like somebody else I know," Amane quipped.

"Huh?"

"Nothing. Something happened this weekend that kind of opened my eyes. I'll clean my place up in a few days."

Itsuki didn't let up. "Nah, man, you gotta sort yourself out *now!*"

Amane turned away in a huff. It would probably take more than half a day to clean that mess up.

Looking exasperated, Itsuki backed off a bit, saying, "I mean, you can live however you want, ya know. But just clear a path you can actually walk through for the next time I come over."

"...I'll deal with it."

Wearing a sour face the whole time, Amane changed into his indoor shoes and headed for his classroom. An extremely boisterous room caught his attention as he walked down a hall, however, and he couldn't help but peek in.

Glancing in through a hallway window, Amane saw Mahiru, as beautiful as she'd ever been, surrounded by her classmates.

Whenever someone spoke to her, she would turn to them with a quiet smile. Everything about her persona seemed totally different from the Mahiru he'd seen the other day. Amane suddenly broke out in a smile.

Noticing his friend's gaze, Itsuki's eyes followed the same path. He saw Mahiru and immediately understood.

"Shiina, huh? As popular as always. No surprise, given how pretty she is."

"Well, you know what they say. She's an angel. What about you, Itsuki? Think she's cute?" Amane asked.

"Yeah, I guess so. But I've got Chi, so only in a sorta aesthetic-appreciation-type way," Itsuki replied.

"Quit going on about your girlfriend already."

Itsuki had a girlfriend named Chi, although that was a nickname. Her full name was Chitose Shirakawa.

They were an extremely close couple, madly in love with each other—it gave Amane heartburn whenever he saw them together.

Although Amane was quick to dismiss the girlfriend talk, Itsuki didn't seem particularly offended. Amane often said things like that, so Itsuki just laughed. "You're heartless. So lemme ask you: Do you think she's cute, Amane?"

"She's definitely beautiful, but that's all," answered Amane.

"How bland," Itsuki commented.

"She's like a flower on a high peak that my hand could never reach. I've got nothing to do with her. Looking is enough."

"Fair."

Some quirk of fate may have brought Mahiru and Amane together that other day, but they were truly destined to live in different worlds.

The idea that Amane, a self-admitted hopeless loser, and Mahiru, the beautiful super-student who could do anything, might one day have any kind of relationship, let alone a romantic one, was frankly ridiculous. It was a veritable impossibility.

That's right, Amane thought. *There's no need to concern myself with her any further.*

"…What are you eating?"

The theory that the two would never interact again was quickly disproven. Amane was sucking down some nutritional jelly on his veranda while gazing up at the sky when Mahiru called to him.

It'd been too much of a bother to even go to the convenience store, so he was contenting himself with the pouch of jelly he had at home while getting some air when Mahiru unexpectedly came out onto her own veranda.

She leaned over her railing slightly, looked at the nutritional jelly pouch that was in Amane's mouth, and frowned.

For a moment, Amane was frozen; he'd thought she was done with him.

"Can't you see? It's a ten-second energy-replenishment jelly," he finally answered.

"...Don't tell me that's what you're calling dinner?" Mahiru asked, incredulous.

"Of course it is."

"That's all you're eating? A high school boy, with a healthy appetite?"

"That's none of your business."

Normally, Amane would've eaten a boxed meal from the convenience store or something premade from the supermarket, but today, he'd neglected to pick something up for dinner, and he didn't feel like instant ramen, so this was all he had. It probably wouldn't be enough, though, so he planned on having a snack later, too.

"...I guess I don't need to ask whether you can cook for yourself. It definitely doesn't seem like you can, at least. And yet you're living on your own, even though you can't cook or clean..." Mahiru's observation was brutally honest.

"Shut up. That's none of your business," Amane fired back, though he knew he couldn't argue with the truth. He frowned and finished off the remainder of his jelly.

He'd wised up about cleaning his place a couple days ago and was definitely planning to do something about it sometime soon. Ruminating on Mahiru's scolding only seemed to make Amane want to do it less, however. It also made him wonder why she was making such a fuss over him in the first place.

Mahiru just stared at Amane, then let out a soft sigh. "…Wait here," she instructed before disappearing back into her own apartment.

"What now?" Amane grumbled as he listened to the clatter of the glass door closing behind her.

He'd been told to wait, but he didn't know what for. Turning a puzzled gaze toward Mahiru's apartment, Amane stood there obediently, but there was no immediate answer.

It's starting to get chilly out here; I'd like to go inside, but…

He'd been told to stay put, so that was what he'd do. The autumn evening was colder than expected, and Amane's loosely fitting, casual clothes did little to help him stay warm.

As Amane waited, watching his deep breaths come out white in the cold, he heard the electronic bell chime from his front door, announcing a visitor. It was pretty obvious who it was.

Truly puzzled, Amane made his way toward the front door, dodging scattered clothes and magazines on the floor.

He knew who it was without even looking through the peephole, so he slid his feet into a pair of slippers, took the chain off the door, and opened it. As expected, he came face-to-face with waves of sandy-blond hair.

"…What are you doing?" Amane asked.

"I couldn't stand how badly you were neglecting your health. These are just some leftovers I had, but please take them," Mahiru stated plainly as she abruptly stuck a hand out in front of her. In her delicate palm, somewhat smaller than Amane's own, was a plastic container. He could vaguely see some sort of stewed dish through the semi-transparent lid. He couldn't tell exactly what it was, however, as the container had filled with steam from the warmth of the food.

Mahiru seemed to understand the confused look in Amane's eyes as he stood there blinking. She let out a deep sigh. "You're not eating properly. Nutritional supplements are just that—supplements. You can't live on them alone."

"What are you, my mom?" Amane jeered.

"I believe what I said is common sense. Also, shouldn't you have tidied up your room by now? There still isn't any room to walk."

Mahiru narrowed her eyes in obvious disappointment as she looked past Amane at the room beyond, and Amane's words stalled in his throat.

"...I have, a little."

"No, you haven't. Normally, people don't drop their clothes on the floor."

"Those just...fell there."

"That wouldn't happen if you washed, dried, folded, and put them away properly. Also, you should bundle up your magazines after you're done reading them. That way you won't slip on one and fall."

It wasn't that he couldn't sense the small barbs in her words, but he also understood that Mahiru was, for some reason, genuinely concerned for him, so he couldn't dismiss everything she was saying. After all, the clutter of magazines had almost tripped the both of them up just the other night. She had a point.

Amane had no rebuttal. He screwed up his face, squeezed his mouth shut tight, and sullenly took the container from Mahiru's hand.

The food suffused his palm with a welcome warmth, especially after all the time spent standing on his chilly veranda.

"So I can eat this?" Amane asked.

"If you don't need it, I can throw it out," Mahiru answered flatly.

"No, I'm grateful for it. I don't usually get to eat an angel's home cooking."

"...Stop calling me that, seriously."

Using her school nickname was a kind of petty, needling revenge for her critical comments. Her feelings about the moniker were written clearly across her pale cheeks as they turned red.

There was no doubt about it—she hated being called an angel. Were he in the same position, Amane was certain he would hate it, too. That hardly needed to be said.

Despite understanding Mahiru's stance, Amane couldn't help but smile when he saw her looking up at him with flushed cheeks and tiny, bitter tears forming.

"I'm not going to say I'm sorry," he declared.

It was clear that any further teasing would be certain to wreck what little goodwill she had left for him, so Amane figured it was prudent to give it a rest.

We're not even that close.

Mahiru also seemed not to want to hear any more, and she emphasized this by clearing her throat forcefully as she pulled herself together.

Her cheeks were still tinged with red, though, so she didn't look like much had changed.

"Well, thank you for this. Though, you don't really need to worry about what happened before," Amane said.

"I don't. I considered that debt settled. This is for my own self-satisfaction… I saw that you weren't taking care of yourself, and I was concerned; that's all."

Of course. Mahiru pitied him; that was it. There was no way to hide—she'd gotten a very good look at how he lived the other night. Even now, she could see the garbage piled up in the hallway behind him.

"You need to at least start eating proper meals and…get your life together!" she scolded.

"Yes, Mom," Amane answered sarcastically. He was getting a little tired of listening to Mahiru's nagging.

Amane churlishly carried the meal Mahiru had brought him back into his apartment. He grabbed a pair of disposable chopsticks he'd gotten at the supermarket and sat down on his living room couch, eager to sample the flavors of her cooking.

He remembered enjoying the rice porridge that she'd brought him before, even though his sense of taste had been dulled by sickness. The slow-cooked porridge had possessed a rich, comforting taste that had been gentle on his stomach. If that was any indication, Mahiru's cooking was undoubtedly quite good, but now it was time to find out for sure.

As he hastily opened the lid of the container, the savory scent of stew drifted gently up at him. Various root vegetables had been cooked together with some chicken. The light-colored sauce underscored the vibrant hues of carrots and green beans, all of which had been cut into bite-size pieces.

Amane's stomach growled, reminding him that the only thing he'd had to eat was some nutritional jelly. He hastily snapped his disposable chopsticks apart and brought a piece of daikon radish to his mouth.

"Yum."

Amane's mouth was greeted with a complex flavor.

Typical of the health-conscious Mahiru, the dish was only lightly seasoned, spiced mostly with dashi stock. It was immediately obvious that she hadn't used store-bought, granulated dashi. Instead, she'd made it herself using with dried bonito fish and kombu seaweed. The difference in taste was night and day.

As he chewed it thoroughly, the flavor of the dashi and the other seasonings, as well as the taste of the vegetables, spread gently through his mouth. Amane had never been a fan of veggies. He usually went out of his way to avoid them, but in this dish, the essence of each ingredient came together in perfect harmony, and Amane happily savored them all.

There wasn't much chicken. Perhaps Mahiru had done that on purpose as if to tell him to eat more vegetables. What little meat there was had been cooked plump and juicy. There was nothing to complain about there, Amane thought, aside from the quantity. For something made by a high school girl, the ingredients were a little plain, but her skill more than made up for it. That Amane so readily enjoyed the food was enough of a testament to that fact.

It would have been even better with some rice, and maybe some miso soup or clear broth on the side, but Amane didn't have any prepared. He was all out of rice anyway, so that modest wish was not destined to be granted that night. It was too late now, but he regretted not buying any instant rice packets beforehand.

"That angel's amazing," Amane said to himself as he devoured the perfectly seasoned vegetables, chopsticks never slowing for a second.

To think, she's great at school, and sports, and all kinds of housework.

If Mahiru had been there to hear Amane's praise, she would have hated it.

"Here's this back. The food was good."

The following evening, Amane carried the borrowed container over to Mahiru's apartment.

The boy was certainly bad at housework, but not so bad that he couldn't wash something before giving it back. In his hand, he held the carefully cleaned little box, knowing that it was good manners to return it only after it had been thoroughly washed and dried.

Mahiru had appeared the moment Amane rang the doorbell without even checking to see who it was, as if she'd been expecting him.

She was wearing a wine-colored knit dress, and when she saw her visitor, her eyes narrowed gently. She quickly checked the container and said, "You washed it and everything, huh? Look at you."

Amane frowned slightly when she praised him like a little child.

"Well, thank you for taking the time," Mahiru continued. "Now take this." She pressed a new, warm container into Amane's hand.

From what he could tell, there was sautéed pork and eggplant inside. It seemed to have cooled enough that the lid hadn't fogged up, for Amane could clearly spy the color of eggplant, grilled pork, and sprinkled sesame seeds through the clear top. From the color, he guessed the sauce was probably miso flavor. The sight of the eggplant with slight scorch marks and the lustrous pork definitely roused his appetite.

No one would deny that it looked delicious, but Amane couldn't understand why he'd been handed dinner again.

"No, um, I just came to return the container," he tried to explain.

"This is today's dinner," Mahiru answered coolly.

"Yeah, I get that, but…"

"I just want to ask: You don't have any allergies, do you? Don't get the wrong idea, though. I won't be catering to your tastes or anything."

"I don't, but… I mean, I can't accept your food again."

Taking a portion of the girl's dinner for the second time in a row seemed wrong to Amane. His malnourished body was grateful for the food, and Mahiru was clearly a much better cook than other girls her age, and the meal he was holding was sure to be delicious, but it also held no small amount of danger.

If someone from school saw the two of them meeting like this, it could turn into a big debacle. That would be the end of Amane's quiet student life for sure.

These apartments were meant for single occupancy, but the rent was pretty high because of the building's location and the amenities. Amane had never seen another student from their school in the building—except Mahiru, of course—so he was probably worrying over nothing. Even with that mild consolation, his brief meetings with the angel still made him wary.

"I made too much, so I'm just happy to be rid of it," Mahiru explained.

"…In that case, I'm happy to take it. But someone might get the wrong idea, since people usually do this sort of thing for someone they like…," Amane said sheepishly.

"And do *you* have the wrong idea?"

"Uh, I guess not."

One look at Mahiru's expression was enough to clear up any misconceptions about her feelings toward Amane.

There was no way that a beautiful, talented girl like Mahiru could possibly fall for an oblivious slob like Amane. Sure, a cute next-door neighbor bringing him food seemed like something out of a romantic comedy, but there was no romance here—and certainly no comedy. The situation was as devoid of those elements as Amane's own apartment was devoid of rice.

What kindness existed in the angel's barbed words had been born only from pity.

"Well then, there's no problem, is there? And anyway, it looks like you were surviving on convenience-store meals and side dishes from the supermarket," stated Mahiru.

"How could you tell?" Amane asked.

"It's not hard to see that your kitchen has barely been used, and you have a ton of disposable chopsticks from the convenience store and the supermarket on your desk. Besides, I can tell just by looking at you. You've got an unhealthy complexion."

Amane's expression froze. Mahiru had gotten all that just from one visit to his apartment. Everything she'd said had been spot-on; he had no room to argue.

"…All right, I'll be going."

Mahiru bowed and went back inside her apartment, having said what she'd wanted to say and given him what she'd wanted to give.

Amane looked at the container in his hands as he listened to the jangling sound of the chain on the other side of Mahiru's front door slide into place. The heat from the food was beginning to warm the palms of his hands. He let out a soft sigh and returned to his place.

As expected, the stir-fried sesame miso eggplant and pork was delicious. Amane found himself wishing even more than yesterday that he'd bought some rice.

As time went on, Amane began swapping an empty container for a full one every day, and his diet improved dramatically.

Mahiru's cooking was always light and healthy, and since every dish made him want rice, Amane started fixing microwave packets with each meal. The angel had a variety of cuisines in her repertoire: Japanese, Chinese, even Western. Each day brought something new, but every single meal was delicious, and Amane developed an appetite like never before.

Like a wild animal grown fat on handouts, Amane quickly came to rely on Mahiru's charity. Even as he continued to obediently accept container after container, he knew it was presumptuous to expect a meal every day. Still, he happily—and hungrily—licked his chops each time.

"…You're looking good lately. You fix your diet or something?"

Itsuki took a long, hard look at Amane one day during lunch. Apparently, his complexion had improved—probably because he was finally supplying his body with much-needed nutrition.

Amane knew his friend was perceptive, and he felt a bit of a cold sweat break out as he slurped the udon noodles he'd ordered for school lunch.

"Itsuki, you scare me," he said.

"Why's that? Do you mean I'm right?"

"Uh, well, I guess you could say I've had no choice but to reexamine my lifestyle recently."

Whenever Amane passed by Mahiru near their apartments, she would chide him gently to take care of himself, and she was regularly sharing her dinner with him. It was only natural that his life had improved. On the one hand, he wanted to call her his guardian angel, but a small part of him also felt like she was meddling where it was none of her business.

Amane had indirectly confirmed Itsuki's suspicions by dodging the question, and Itsuki cackled with delighted laughter. "Yeah, I knew it. You always looked unhealthy 'cause the way you were living was so crappy."

"Shut up."

"But what made you decide to 'reexamine your lifestyle'?"

"I guess I was forced to."

"Ah, your mom found out?"

"...You're not right, but you're not far off, either."

Mahiru really did sound like Amane's mom at times. She was much too young and too cute to be a mother, though. Still, the way the girl went to such lengths to care for Amane made it hard for him to refuse her.

"Say, Itsuki? Do I really seem that unhealthy?"

"Hmm... Well, to start with, you're pretty pale. I guess you're tall enough, but you're gangly. You're also always shuffling around all apathetic-like, so you look like a zombie."

"But that's just how I look..."

"You think I don't know that? Try looking like one of the living for a change."

"Don't be absurd... Wait, but seriously...a zombie...?"

Amane wasn't really sure because he almost never bothered to closely check his own face in the mirror, but apparently, he gave others the impression that he was barely alive. If he looked half-dead even on a good day, that would explain why Mahiru had been so worried about him before.

"You should pay a little more attention to how other people see you, Amane. You're always hunched over, starin' at the ground. It makes you hard to approach, and it's not like you go out of your way to get close to anybody, either. If I didn't know any better, I'd say you're the very definition of a moody teenager."

"You sure know how to keep it casual when you're insulting a guy."

"Fine, fine, I won't sugarcoat it, then. You look like a corpse, and your life is a mess." Itsuki continued teasing his friend, insisting that he ought to take this opportunity to pay more attention to his appearance and demeanor, not to mention his health.

Sharply turning away, Amane replied sarcastically, "Thanks for your concern."

A Chance Encounter

"Ah."

Amane heard a beautiful voice ring out like a bell from behind him.

Recently, he'd grown accustomed to hearing that voice, but only around his apartment building. Now he heard it while he was standing in the sweets aisle at the neighborhood supermarket.

Amane had never expected Mahiru to acknowledge him in public, so he turned around with some bewilderment to see her standing there, eyes wide.

A supermarket basket hung from her arm, and inside it sat a daikon radish and some tofu, as well as a package of chicken thighs and a carton of milk. These were likely the ingredients for her dinner tonight.

This was nothing special. Amane had coincidentally stopped by the candy aisle at the same time. That was all.

"Just so you know, this is merely a coincidence," Amane asserted. "It's not like I'm stalking you or anything."

"I know, I know." Mahiru nodded. "We're both just here because it's the closest supermarket." Before Amane had a chance to agree, he heard the girl mutter, "Really, though, that's the first thing that came to mind...?" She stared down at a notebook that she was carrying.

It was just like the meticulous Mahiru to dutifully record everything she needed. Ignoring Amane in favor of her flower-patterned notebook, Mahiru brushed past the sweets and began searching the condiments on display in the next aisle.

Something about Mahiru searching the shelves for kitchen staples and murmuring things like *soy sauce* and *mirin* in her lovely voice seemed cute to Amane. It was clear that the girl was in a strange kind of mood, however.

"Mirin is right here. Look," Amane said, pointing it out.

"Ah, not that—I'm looking for the low-alcohol kind. I can't buy that, since I'm underage," Mahiru replied.

"This is considered alcohol?"

"Mirin is sweet rice wine, after all. The ones that are specifically for cooking still have alcohol, but they add in salt to make it gross to drink, so even underage people can buy it."

Amane had been about to hand her a bottle of mirin when she suddenly refused it, shook her head, and instead placed the low-alcohol alternative in her basket.

"Learn something every day..." This was all new to Amane, who did so little housework that even these simple tidbits seemed revelatory. He watched Mahiru as she moved quickly on down the aisle, stopping in front of a shelf full of soy sauce.

Mahiru frowned, as if she had only just noticed the price labels. "...Bargain price, limit one bottle per person..." She had apparently been intending to buy a spare. Mahiru grumbled in disappointment and turned to glance at Amane.

"Maybe...I could buy one, too?" Amane quickly sensed what Mahiru had been trying to convey with her eyes, and with a wry smile, he picked up a bottle of soy sauce. When he did, her lips formed a satisfied arch.

"It's helpful to have someone who understands," she said.

"...You're more economical than I expected," Amane commented.

"Well, I don't see why I shouldn't find the best prices when I can. Cut down on needless expense, right?"

"I wonder if that's what they call a thrifty mentality. Well, as long as you're living on an allowance from your parents, I guess that's for the best."

Amane may have technically lived alone, but in reality, his parents still supported him. His family was fairly rich, and they covered the rent of his clean, safe apartment, took care of his school fees, and provided him with a more-than-fair allowance. Amane had never had to worry about his expenses, but he was grateful for everything his parents did for him, so he tried not to waste money.

"...That's right. We depend on their support, so it's important to be frugal," Mahiru replied matter-of-factly, taking stock of the contents of her basket. Her voice was cold, like something had stolen away her warmth.

Amane flinched at Mahiru's flat tone, but when she looked up from her groceries, her expression had returned to normal. The gloomy eyes he'd seen in that brief moment were already gone.

"...Anyway, are you really buying that?" Mahiru asked, as if to change the subject, looking at the packs of instant rice and the container of potato salad that were in the basket that Amane was holding.

The meals that Mahiru was sharing with him were, of course, delicious, but they weren't enough on their own. To compensate, Amane would pick up a staple food and side salad like he'd done today.

"I mean, it's dinner," Amane explained.

"It's unhealthy," Mahiru shot back.

"You're so fussy. I'm buying a salad, aren't I?"

"A *potato* salad... How is your body still functioning?"

"Mind your own business."

Mahiru put wordless pressure on him, scrutinizing him with eyes that reproached him and told him to eat more vegetables. Amane turned away and let Mahiru go ahead of him.

Chatting about this and that, the two bought their respective things. Amane had started to pack his purchases into a plastic bag, but Mahiru produced a reusable bag she'd brought and quickly put everything into it.

She was truly an environmentally conscious angel.

Mahiru had only brought the one bag, however, and Amane was a little anxious that the quantity of groceries was too much for it.

With the milk, soy sauce, and low-alcohol cooking mirin, that was four liters of liquid altogether, and if they weighed anything like water, that meant four kilograms right there. There was still the whole daikon radish and the other ingredients to consider, too. The bag had to be really heavy. Everything was packed in quite neatly, but still, it would surely be hard work carrying it all the way back to Amane and Mahiru's building.

She's been cooking for me, so she must be going through more seasonings and ingredients than she normally does.

She's gotta be making a lot in order to split the dishes with me. The amount she gives me is always nearly a whole meal's worth. Mahiru says it's all just extra, but she must be making a lot of food on purpose.

After Mahiru had gone through so much trouble to take care of Amane, it'd wound his pride if he didn't do anything to help her out now.

As soon as Mahiru finished packing the reusable bag, Amane took hold of the handles and lifted it. It wasn't all that heavy to him, of course, but he could tell that it would definitely be difficult for her to carry for very long.

Mahiru may have been really good at sports, but pure arm strength was an entirely different matter. Surely, Amane thought, his eyes tracing her slim figure under her clothing, surely there was no way that her slender arms could command the power needed to lift these heavy groceries.

Caramel-colored eyes blinked rapidly. Mahiru looked surprised— or maybe a little concerned.

"…I'm not stealing it or anything," Amane said in his defense.

"I'm not worried about that," Mahiru replied. "It's just…I can carry my own bags, you know?"

"It'd be more charming if you'd be quiet and let me take care of you for a change," quipped Amane.

"That's basically saying I'm not charming," Mahiru answered flatly.

"Well, think about how you act at school, then compare that to how you act toward me."

Mahiru took a step back. Maybe Amane had unknowingly hit a nerve. The version of herself that she showed at school—the kind, gentle, modest girl everyone was familiar with—that was not the person Amane knew. Yes, Mahiru was always kind to him, but she was also far more direct. She never sugarcoated anything or hid behind niceties. Everything she said to him was brief and frank.

Amane took advantage of Mahiru's stunned silence and briskly sauntered off toward the supermarket exit, holding his schoolbag in one hand and the reusable shopping bag stuffed with groceries in the other. He was leaving her behind, but he didn't care. Unconcerned, he continued on as the gap between them grew wider. He didn't slow down or give her a chance to catch up.

They had already been standing next to each other in the

supermarket, after all. If they walked side by side on the way home and somebody saw them, that could start rumors.

So really, this kind of distance was best for both of them.

Amane hurried on with his heavy burden while pretending not to be aware of Mahiru.

As he strode along, he thought he heard someone mutter "Thanks" behind him.

Chapter 5

The Angel and the Great Cleaning Campaign

Amane was terrible at housework of any kind, but the thing he was worst at was cleaning.

Surprisingly, he actually could cook. More specifically, he could prepare something hot and usually technically edible, as long as he was willing to set aside petty concerns like presentation or flavor and also assumed the possibility of grievous bodily injury at some point during the process. He wasn't completely incapable of preparing food.

Laundry was all right, too. That much was possible for anyone, even Amane. If push came to shove, there was always the option of taking his clothes to a coin laundromat. All it boiled down to was a matter of stuffing everything into the machine and letting it run with detergent and water inside. Amane could pull that off, no problem. The one thing he was absolutely hopeless with, however, was cleaning.

"What do I do?"

One weekend, Amane had finally gotten tired of listening to both Mahiru and Itsuki lecture him day in and day out about cleaning his apartment and had resolved to finally do something about it. The only problem was that Amane was at a complete loss on how to get started.

He knew that this was his own fault, but the first problem was that his things were piled up all over the place, and he couldn't figure out how he could even begin to get them in order. Unsure of what else to do, Amane started by washing his bedsheets and airing out his futon.

What should come next? he wondered. *Clothes and magazines are scattered everywhere, so there's really no room to walk.*

One small mercy was that he always threw out any food garbage right away, so there were no awful stenches or greasy stains. It was simply an enormous amount of clutter—enough that it seemed like an insurmountable problem.

As Amane sighed softly at the mountain of work before him, the doorbell rang. He let out a little gasp.

Rather than a regular visitor, he had begun to think of his neighbor more like a delivery person, a blessing from above who just handed over gifts and then left. As he stood before his messy room, however, Mahiru seemed like a savior.

Amane scrambled for his front door but couldn't find his footing. He stumbled, caught himself, and carefully crept the rest of the way to the door with one hand pressed against the wall for balance.

"Sorry, I wanted to pick up my container a little earlier today… What are you doing?" Mahiru asked when Amane opened the door.

"…I was trying to clean," he admitted.

Mahiru looked at Amane, still off-balance, with a rather astonished expression.

"I heard a loud noise just now," she said.

"…I almost fell."

"I bet you did. You haven't even begun to clean, have you?"

"I wasn't sure how to start."

"I can tell."

Amane grimaced at Mahiru's comment. It was no less candid than usual, and Amane really couldn't think of anything to justify his lack of progress. Besides, he knew that if he got sulky now and lashed out, he wouldn't be able to get her advice on how to go about cleaning his apartment. The trouble was that he wasn't sure how exactly to ask for Mahiru's help.

I was hoping for some cleaning tips, but I wonder if she'll actually give me any advice...

Amane hesitated when he saw that Mahiru was peering past him at the clutter beyond. Her eyes conveyed her shock at the disastrous scene behind him. It truly must've been an awful sight.

"Unbelievable... I'll help you clean your apartment."

"Huh?"

Even Amane knew that it would be too shameless to ask Mahiru to help him clean. That's why he'd only been planning to see if she had any suggestions. Never had he dared to imagine that Mahiru would come right out and offer to help.

"I hate the idea that the apartment next to mine is so filthy." Such scathing words, but again, Amane could offer no argument. "You must think it's so easy to live alone, but you can't even clean up after yourself. Worse, you act like it's no problem, like everything will sort itself out eventually, but it clearly hasn't. Why don't you stop and take a moment to look at yourself?"

Amane was at a loss for words. His mother had always told him that if he was diligent about cleaning regularly, it would be easy, but he'd ignored her, and this was the result. He was fully aware that he was suffering the consequences of his own actions.

"Look, as long as you keep up with routine cleaning, your place won't get this bad again. It's obvious that you have some terrible habits," Mahiru said.

"...You're absolutely right," agreed Amane.

He couldn't get angry with her. He already owed her so much, and she'd been so kind to him. Besides, everything she was saying

about his past behavior was true. He *had* underestimated how difficult living alone would be, and he really did just sort of assume that
everything would somehow work itself out, and *this* was the result.
Amane could only nod solemnly at Mahiru's words.

"Well, is it all right if I start with this room?" Mahiru asked.

"...Is it all right with you?" Amane answered with a question of
his own.

"I'm the one who's offering, so of course it's all right. I'm going to
go get ready, so while I do, if you have anything you don't want me to
see, or any valuables, please put them in a closet and lock them up."

"I'm not worried about that."

Amane refused to even entertain the idea that someone who had
been so kind to him, even despite her sharp words, might steal from
him. Not to mention that Mahiru was far too good-hearted to ever
harm another person like that.

"...You're not?" she inquired.

"There's no way that you would do something like that," Amane
replied.

"No, that's not what I... Look, aren't you worried that I might see
something that, as a boy, you'd rather hide?"

"Ah...uh, well, unfortunately I don't happen to have any such
things."

"Well, in that case, it's fine, then. All right, I'm going to go
change clothes and fetch some cleaning supplies. I don't take cleaning lightly, you know."

Mahiru returned to her apartment, and Amane watched her go
with a wry smile.

She came back wearing different clothes: a long white T-shirt and
khaki-colored cargo pants. The T-shirt closely followed the lines of

her body, the delicate fabric bringing the curves and edges into full relief. Mahiru's long hair had been skillfully gathered into a perfectly round bun, and Amane felt strangely uncomfortable being able to see the white nape of her neck.

Previously, he had only ever seen her in dresses and skirts, and he found there was something refreshing about this look. Amane had thought before that boyish clothes like this probably wouldn't suit her well, but he had clearly been wrong. He was beginning to realize that beautiful girls looked good in whatever they put on.

This new outfit looked comfortable for moving around the house, but it was also a look that Mahiru could've worn around town. Amane never would've imagined that these were clothes that she was okay with getting dirtied.

"You don't mind if those get messed up?" Amane asked.

"I was planning to throw these out soon anyway, so it's fine if they get a bit dirty." Mahiru scanned the cataclysm that was Amane's apartment and sighed softly. "I'm only going to say this once: We're going to clean *thoroughly*, got it?"

"...I understand."

"Good, then let's get to it. I'm not going to go easy on you, and I won't let this end halfway through. I assume you have no objections?" Mahiru had posed the question so forcefully that Amane could do nothing but sheepishly reply in the affirmative.

So began the great battle to clean Amane's apartment. A battle spearheaded by an angel.

"First things first, let's toss any clothes into the laundry basket. Usually when you clean, you work from top to bottom, but we have to handle the clutter on the floor first before we can run the vacuum cleaner. Before we start the wash, we can divide the clothes into different loads, since there are too many to wash at once. Do you want to split them into things you wear and things you don't wear? Or do you want to wash everything?"

"Just do it however you like…," replied Amane. It seemed so obvious to him now. Of course they had to clear the floor before trying to do anything else.

"…There isn't any underwear out here or anything, right?"

"Those are in my dresser, as you would expect."

"That's fine, then. We can probably put off washing clothes for now, since even if we wash and dry them, we'll kick up dust by cleaning and just end up having to do them again. If you're not in a hurry, you can do the laundry after we finish cleaning."

"Okay."

"…Now, regarding the magazines. Really, the only thing to do is to throw them out. I suppose it's a bit of a different story if you're collecting them, but from the way you keep them piled up everywhere, I doubt that's the case. If you do want to hold on to some part of one, tear out the page and put it in a scrapbook, then dispose of the rest. Tie up any magazines you're getting rid of and put them out for collection."

Mahiru set about the task of cleaning right away, directing Amane to put his discarded clothing into the laundry basket as she gathered up every last magazine. She told him to speak now if there were any that Amane wanted to keep, but there weren't any in particular that he needed, so he simply shook his head. Having received the answer she required, Mahiru skillfully tied up the bundle using some plastic cord that she had apparently brought with her.

"When you're finished gathering the clothes, please go through the other assorted clutter and decide whether to throw anything out. All these different things on the floor: same as before, sort them into what you need to keep and what you don't. Then put the latter in the trash. Got it?"

"...Uh-huh," Amane answered meekly.

"If you have a problem with taking orders, you'd better tell me now."

"No, I don't, but...I was just thinking about how quick you're doing all of this."

"If I don't, we'll run out of time. It's total chaos in here, after all."

"You're right."

Even though it was the weekend, time was limited. If they were going to run the vacuum, it would have to be during the day, considering that the noise would be a nuisance to the neighbors. Since Mahiru knew that it would take a lot of effort to get the place to a state where they could vacuum, she was working to tidy up as quickly as possible.

One part of Amane felt bad for letting her do so much. On the other hand, under Mahiru's direction, more and more of the floor began to appear for the first time in a long while.

"Professor Shiina...," Amane muttered.

"If you're going to ask for guidance from me like I'm a teacher, first learn by imitating. I'm not going to sort through your personal effects, so please be diligent and keep only what you really need," Mahiru instructed.

"Yes, sir."

"Please don't address me as a man."

The angel nonchalantly returned Amane's jabs as she skillfully cleared up more of the clutter with a serious expression the whole time.

Amane had a bad habit of hoarding useless junk, and he was both grateful for Mahiru's decisiveness and envious of it. Here she was, in a stranger's apartment, picking through the mess without hesitation. She really was the spitting image of an angel.

Mahiru was so efficient that she could have easily cleaned up the whole place by herself had she wanted to. However, likely because she was in such a hurry, she got careless about watching her footing. There was no doubt that it was Amane's fault for leaving it on the floor, but Mahiru slipped on a piece of discarded clothing and lost her balance.

The instant a small "Ah!" escaped Mahiru's mouth, Amane dived across the room, aiming for the spot where he thought Mahiru would most likely fall.

A light, sweet fragrance mixed with the musty smell of the dust that had been kicked up in the panic.

Amane landed on his backside, leaving his rear end to suffer a dull sting, but it was tolerable. He groaned just a bit as he felt the weight of Mahiru pressing down on him.

She must be happy that I caught her right away.

"...Fujimiya?" Mahiru looked up at him. She didn't seem angry, but she didn't seem particularly happy about the situation, either. Mostly, she just sounded surprised. "I can accept the blame for falling, but this is exactly why you must tidy up, because otherwise things like this are bound to happen."

"I'm really sorry, honestly... You're not hurt, are you?" Amane asked.

"I'm fine. Thanks for going out of your way to catch me. I'm sorry, too."

"No, it's all my fault..."

Amane wouldn't have been able to bear it if Mahiru had gotten hurt while helping him, especially considering she was already sharing meals with him. That would've been absolutely unforgivable; he wouldn't have even been able to look her in the eye.

If he needed to, he was considering kneeling and asking for forgiveness, but Mahiru didn't seem too upset over her tumble.

"We're cleaning up so that things like this don't happen anymore, understand?"

"Yeah. I'm really very sorry."

"It's fine; you don't need to apologize. I'm helping you because I feel like it, after all." Mahiru looked just a little bit flustered as she gazed up at Amane.

Amane suddenly realized how close they were and was aware of her pressing against him. For a boy who basically never interacted with girls on a regular basis, this was a heart-pounding situation. Even though neither of them had any romantic feelings for the other, something felt very wrong about it somehow.

Mahiru didn't seem to be conscious of the situation, so Amane gently grabbed her shoulder and pushed her off of him; then he stood up before the awkwardness could show on his face.

"…Should we…keep cleaning?" he managed after a moment.

"Yes, that's a good idea," Mahiru replied. Fortunately for Amane, she appeared to be oblivious to his trembling as she grabbed the hand Amane extended and rose to her feet.

Mahiru seemed unaware of how closely she'd been pressed up against him, because she just maintained her usual expression. Amane figured that a girl like Mahiru must've been used to the attention of a lot of boys. Surely a little contact like that wouldn't be enough to unnerve her like it did him.

Smiling wryly at Mahiru's demeanor, Amane decided it would be wrong to leave everything up to her and returned to cleaning with newfound resolve. Even though the task was wholly unfamiliar, he did his best to struggle through.

"…You are full of surprises."

Amane was too focused on his work to notice the quiet words that escaped Mahiru's lips, nor did he see that her ears, hidden by her straw-colored hair, had turned slightly red.

✳　　✳　　✳

"...Whew, now, this is clean."

In the end, it had taken the pair the entire day to clean Amane's apartment.

Several hours were spent tidying up the clutter on his floor, and then, between washing the clothes, dusting the shelves and light fixtures, scrubbing the windows, and vacuuming, the entire day had flown by before they knew it.

The sun had been visible when Mahiru came over, but it had long since set by now, proof of just how long she and Amane had been working.

It had certainly been no small task, but those efforts were not without results. Amane's apartment was so clean that he barely recognized it. There was no unnecessary clutter, and he could see the floor! Once-dirty windowpanes and frames didn't have a single speck of dirt on them. The lights, too, shone brighter now that they had been dusted. The place was finally clean. Without all the junk crowding every surface, it actually looked to be quite a comfortable space.

"To think that it took us a whole day," Mahiru observed.

"Guess that's what it takes when it's such a mess...," Amane answered.

"But it was *your* mess."

"R-right you are."

Amane verbally prostrated himself before his angelic savior, who had taken mercy on him. Mahiru, who had wasted one of her precious weekend days helping him, finished tying up a garbage bag with a beleaguered look. She didn't seem upset, but a hint of fatigue showed on her face, though it was mixed with a sense of accomplishment. That was only natural, since she had been working all day.

After everything that had transpired, Amane would have been ashamed to simply let Mahiru go make dinner. It'd be unforgivable to expect her to do any more work, whether she shared a portion of her cooking with him today or not.

"Now that it's evening, I don't feel like going shopping, so I'm going to order a pizza or something. Please let me treat you today. After all, you've been giving me all kinds of food and stuff," Amane offered.

"Oh, but—," Mahiru started, but she was quickly cut off.

"If you don't want to eat with me, I'll order one for you, and you can take it home."

This gesture was more about showing gratitude than trying to get Mahiru to eat with him, so if she wanted to eat alone, Amane didn't mind.

"…That's not what I meant. It's just… I was surprised, because I've never ordered pizza."

"Huh, you've never ordered pizza?"

"Yeah, I live alone, but I've never ordered pizza… I've made it myself, though."

"It's amazing that you would even think to make it," Amane exclaimed.

Normally, if someone decided they wanted pizza, the three options were to buy a ready-made one at the store, get it delivered, or go eat it in a restaurant. He was sure that there were very few people who would think to go through the long, laborious process of making one from scratch.

"Well, there's nothing strange about ordering pizza for delivery," Amane asserted. "I do it all the time myself: order delivery or go to a family restaurant solo…you know, like most people."

"I've actually never been to one of those, either," Mahiru admitted.

"Now, *that* is rare. I go alone pretty often, and my parents go to restaurants whenever they don't feel like cooking. I guess your parents aren't the type to eat out often, huh?"

"...In our house, the help made the meals."

"The help? Damn, you must be really rich."

Finding out that Mahiru was fabulously wealthy explained a lot. It certainly cleared up why Mahiru's mannerisms were so graceful and refined—and why her clothes and possessions were always top quality. Even the girl's gait seemed to speak of an affluent upbringing.

At Amane's words, Mahiru broke into a thin smile. "You're right; I think I am comparatively well-off."

Quickly, Amane began to regret what he'd said, realizing that Mahiru's smile was not one of delight or pride but rather a display of self-mockery. It seemed that her family was an area of discussion that was better left alone, and Amane didn't plan to pry any further.

Everybody has a thing or two they'd rather not talk about. It's only polite to respect that, especially with people you don't know very well.

"Well, then this will be an interesting experience, won't it? Here, order what you like."

Dropping the topic of Mahiru's parents, Amane showed her a menu for a pizza place Amane occasionally ordered from. Out of all the places that delivered, it was the best. Their pizza was no match for one cooked in an authentic wood-fired oven, of course, but they did offer a wide variety of toppings. Their choices ranged from the standard fare to stuff more suited to little kids, so Amane figured that there was sure to be something that would appeal to Mahiru's tastes.

Mahiru accepted both the change of subject and the pizza menu. She immediately began poring over the list of options, her luminous brown eyes drawn to the many colorful photos of different pizzas. Her eyes weren't usually very expressive, but now they shimmered vividly.

She must really be looking forward to this, Amane thought.

Mahiru seemed a bit nervous, but after considering it for a little while, she pointed out a party pizza with four types of toppings and said hesitantly, "All right, this looks good." She turned an expectant gaze to Amane.

With a slight smile, Amane nodded, picked up his phone, and dialed the number printed on the menu. Mahiru's eyes sparkled with anticipation.

An hour later, their pizza arrived. Mahiru dug in without hesitation. The pizza was divided into sections to allow the different flavors to be sampled on their own, and she'd hesitated a little over which one to try first but finally decided to start with a piece covered with a hearty helping of bacon and sausage.

Amane was not surprised when Mahiru nibbled at her slice with small, delicate bites. He supposed her refined upbringing had taught her to eat everything with poise and grace, even delivery pizza.

Watching Mahiru gave Amane a warm feeling inside, like he was watching a small, cute animal. She was strangely adorable as her eyes closed and her expression relaxed a little while she chewed on the stretchy cheese. Usually, the girl appeared so mature; in this moment, however, she finally looked her age.

Amane quelled an intense urge to pat Mahiru's head as she enjoyed the pizza with little, mincing bites.

"…What?" she asked.

"Nothing, you just look like you're enjoying it," Amane replied.

"Please don't stare at me so much."

The frown she cast at Amane was anything but cute, however.

"…Geez, you've really got no charm."

"Well, that suits me fine. If I were to act like I always do at school, you'd say I was making you uncomfortable."

"Yeah, I guess that's true. I'm more familiar with this version of you than the school version."

At school, Amane barely ever even saw Mahiru, and they had certainly never spoken there. He only occasionally caught a glimpse of her, and she always wore that same, impenetrable smile that she showed to everyone.

Here, he got to see beyond that layer. *This has to be the real Mahiru,* Amane thought. At school, she always adopted her fake, public persona.

"As far as I'm concerned," he continued, "I never get tired of this version."

"The version with no charm?"

"Don't hold a grudge... You know, how do I put this...? I can never tell what you're thinking when you're at school."

"Mostly about my schedule and my classes, I suppose."

"So even you can be clueless once in a while, huh?"

Amane had meant to say that Mahiru always looked like she had some secret on her mind, but Mahiru apparently took his words at face value. She looked at him with a subtle protest in her eyes, as though she had meant something else entirely.

"I, uh, didn't mean it like that," Amane quickly added. "It's just... You don't show what you're thinking. All I meant was that it's easier to be around someone who's honest about their feelings, even if they're a little rude, than someone who you can never read."

"...Do you think how I behave at school is bad?" Mahiru asked directly.

"Well, I can't really hate on it, since it's probably the secret to your success. I just wonder if you ever get tired of it," Amane said.

"Not really. I've been acting like that since I was little."

"Hard-core, huh?"

If she'd been keeping up this act since childhood, spending her whole life trying to be the perfect young woman everyone expected her to be, Amane could understand how it would definitely be difficult for her to set that persona aside.

Amane had been able to infer a little bit about Mahiru's home life, but he knew that there was no way he could ask her more about it.

"Well, isn't it nice to have a place where you can relax? And now you've even got a buddy to chill with."

"Honestly, I don't find you relaxing at all. You make my stomach turn in knots," Mahiru stated coldly.

"I'm…sorry?" Amane apologized, a little dumbstruck.

Mahiru gave an exaggerated shrug and let out a strange little laugh.

Chapter 6

A Visit from a Friend

After the day-long cleanup, Amane felt like the wall between Mahiru and him had become ever-so-slightly thinner, but that didn't necessarily mean they had become much closer.

They still had absolutely zero contact at school; they would make small talk sometimes when he went to get his portion of dinner from her, but that was all.

Just the other day, Mahiru had scolded Amane, telling him that he had to keep his apartment tidy. Her words were definitely stern, but they also made it clear that she actually did care about him, at least a bit.

Since Amane was receiving frequent reminders and tips on cleaning, his apartment remained as nice as it had been when he and Mahiru had finished tidying up the place.

"Wow, it really is clean." That was the first thing Itsuki said when he came over on a day off. He muttered in an astonished voice when he saw the drastic transformation the living room had undergone.

"I never thought your place could look this good. It was so dirty. I remember I helped you pick up stuff once before, but it was a wreck the very next day."

"Give it a rest," Amane shot back at his friend.

"No, but seriously, think about it. What's the longest number of days you've gone without dropping something on your floor?"

"This is easily a new record. I've kept it going for two weeks."

"Two weeks?! That's it? That's nothing to be proud of, you know?"

Amane scowled a little. He was now keenly aware that normally, people did not leave their things lying around on the floor. Still, he knew that Itsuki was only speaking from a place of kindness and common sense, so Amane couldn't say much. After all, Itsuki had helped him out, too, long before Mahiru ever had, so Amane knew he shouldn't act like a jerk.

Itsuki smiled cheerfully at Amane's sullen silence. "Hey, I guess if your apartment's this clean, I could even bring Chi over."

"No way; why should I have to watch you two flirting in my own home?"

"No need to be shy, buddy."

"Don't turn my place into your hangout!"

Why should I have to watch my friend and his girlfriend getting all lovey-dovey?

Amane wished Itsuki could understand his position and appreciate what kind of torture it was like to have to watch a sickeningly sweet couple flirting all the time. He knew that Itsuki was just joking about bringing Chi over, but even so, Amane didn't find it very amusing that he constantly had front-row seats to their cloying relationship.

"Relax, it was just a joke. Anyway, now that you've finally got the place clean, don't go messing it up again, you hear?"

"I've got it under control," Amane assured.

"Someone like you... Well, whatever. Just make sure you get in the habit of putting things away after you take them out."

"Are you my mom...?"

"Now, Amane, dearie, you have to be diligent about cleaning your room!" Itsuki mocked.

"That's so creepy; you sound so much like my mom, it's scary!"

Amane felt a shiver rocket down his back when Itsuki scolded him in a forced falsetto.

He was sure Itsuki had never even met his mother, but still, the impression had hit a nerve. Itsuki's impersonation of a lady wasn't particularly soothing, either. Amane stuck out his tongue at him, and Itsuki cackled with amusement.

"Is that what your mom's like, Amane? Because mine is really cold toward me…"

"Actually, I'm jealous. My mom bugs me whenever she gets the chance."

"She sounds like a mom who really cares about her son."

"I think she's just overly attached…"

"No, I'm sure she has to look after you because you're such a slob."

"Oh, shut up. I mean it, you know, that my mom is too clingy."

Perhaps because Amane was an only child, his mother was always fussing over him.

She didn't exactly spoil him, but she did poke her nose around in his business and read too much into things. Amane certainly didn't hate her, but she made him uncomfortable at times.

His mother had given him all sorts of instructions when he'd left home to live on his own and attend high school, and sometimes she would show up to check on him without warning. The pop-ins could be pretty awful.

"Well, doesn't that just show how much she treasures you, Amane?"

"And her love is a heavy burden."

"Oh, I give up. You're the kind of guy who never appreciates what he's got till it's gone."

"You talk like you've got it all figured out, but don't you have your own problems dealing with that kind of meddling?"

"Ha-ha! It's Chi, man; what else can I do?" Itsuki had all sorts of issues when it came to his father and his girlfriend, so his lecture really didn't have much weight behind it. Even so, Amane knew there was some truth to what his friend was saying, so he didn't argue any further.

Itsuki sighed quietly, as if to tell Amane to let him worry about his own problems. His expression remained cheerful and carefree, however. "I'll mess up anybody who interferes with me and Chi!" Itsuki said, declaring something a little unsettling. "Anyway, I'll figure out something for my dad situation, so it's all good. For the time being, how 'bout you sort your life out, Amane?"

Itsuki laughed loudly, and Amane responded by making a sour face. "I know that; you don't have to tell me." He smiled secretly to himself, however, thinking how he'd heard that before from another person recently.

Itsuki had come to visit Amane's apartment in order to see how he was living. Well, actually, he'd mostly come to hang out and mess around, so their discussion about the state of the room quickly wrapped up, and before long, they were playing a video game. Their initial intention had been to study for a test the next week, but that notion had been quickly discarded.

"Careful with the health packs; we're gonna run out," Amane said.

"We'll think of something; it'll be fine," Itsuki answered.

"Not at this level it won't..."

As Amane pondered how best to deal with his less cautious co-op player, the sound of the doorbell rang through the room and immediately gave rise to a different worry.

"Hmm? A visitor?"

Itsuki looked up, too, after pausing the game. He knew that Amane had never really told anyone else where he lived, and that he didn't have any friends who might visit him at home, besides Itsuki himself. More importantly, any regular visitor would have been stopped at the lobby downstairs anyway, so a page should have come through the intercom.

"I don't really know, but it must be a neighbor, right? Distributing a community notice or something," Amane fibbed, knowing quite well who it likely was.

"Ah, gotcha," Itsuki answered.

"I'll just be a minute."

Amane did his best to dispel Itsuki's suspicions and hurried toward the front door, struggling to hide the twitch in his face that might give him away. He was lucky that Mahiru hadn't called out to him after ringing the buzzer.

He opened the door quickly, not bothering to check who it was, and slipped through the small opening to get outside where he couldn't be seen. Amane made sure to close the door behind himself.

Just as he'd suspected, it was Mahiru standing there, blinking in surprise at Amane, who must have appeared to have been acting very unusual.

Immediately, he pressed an index finger to his lips and shushed Mahiru. "...Please speak softly. Itsuki is here."

"Itsuki?" she asked.

"My friend. He came over to play games."

"Ah, okay."

Mahiru nodded in understanding of Amane's secretive behavior, then passed him a food container as she did every day without bothering to question him any further.

Inside was a type of stew called *oden*, the perfect dish for the season now that the weather had gotten cold. Mahiru had probably been preparing it since morning. Amane accepted it with gratitude and let out a soft sigh as he looked at Mahiru. There was really no reason she ought to be doing this every day.

"Look, I really appreciate what you do, but…I don't have a lot of time. Sorry," Amane apologized.

"I wasn't waiting to be thanked or anything… I'm glad, you know, that we cleaned up enough that you can invite friends over," Mahiru answered.

"I guess I should kneel down and thank you."

"No way; don't do that."

Mahiru looked at him with astonishment in her eyes. Perhaps she thought getting Amane to do something like that would make her akin to a tyrant. Amane smiled wryly.

There had been a bit of earnestness in his statement, because he truly was indebted to her. She'd done so much for him that he really ought to be on his knees. Amane couldn't reconcile continuing to accept all the food for free, so he decided that he wanted to discuss paying her for the meals at some later date.

"Well, if your friend is here, I suppose you can't talk for too long. Excuse me."

"…You're always helping me out. I'll make sure to keep this secret from Itsuki."

"Please do."

"I mean, even if I told him everything, he probably won't believe me."

"I suppose not."

Mahiru's honest confirmation raised some complex feelings for

Amane, but he knew she was right. If he was in Itsuki's shoes and someone told him that Mahiru Shiina had been making meals for him daily, he definitely wouldn't believe them. Anyone would dismiss such a claim as a fantasy.

That was how out of reach this angel was.

Normally, it would be impossible to imagine Mahiru treating even a handsome, superior man to her home cooking, let alone a mediocre and slovenly guy like Amane. Hell would sooner freeze over.

"...Can I ask you one thing?" Amane called.

"What is it?" Mahiru stopped before entering her apartment.

"What good does it do you to keep sharing your meals with me?"

Typically, people didn't give away food for free—they expected something in return. Amane probably wouldn't have thought about doing the same for Mahiru if their positions had been reversed. Even though he didn't believe for a moment that there was even the slightest possibility that she had feelings for him, he couldn't help but wonder.

At Amane's question, Mahiru gaze wandered upward as if she was giving it a bit of thought herself, then, without any change to her expression, answered, "My own self-satisfaction. There's nothing more to it. It's just as easy for me to cook for two people as it is for one, and I guess I simply like treating people."

"So it's because you like to cook?"

"Well, there's that, too. I think it's also because I can give you food without you getting any weird ideas, and you'll genuinely tell me that my cooking's tasty without any ulterior motives. Plus, it's satisfying for me because I was concerned after seeing your eating habits."

"...Is that how it is?" Amane pressed, just the slightest bit disappointed.

"That's how it is. So don't worry about it. Just think of it as...a sudden bout of good fortune."

"Yes, ma'am."

Mahiru didn't seem like she was going to give him any more of an answer than that, and after bowing courteously, she said "Pardon me" and returned to her own apartment.

"I guess that's how it goes," Amane mumbled to himself. "I still don't think it's right for her to give it to me for free, though." He opened the door back into his own place.

"Who was it?" Itsuki asked.

"My neighbor. She gave me some of her dinner. I'm gonna put it in the fridge, so don't restart the game without me," Amane replied.

"Ah, sorry, I already beat the boss."

"You gotta be kidding me."

Chapter 7

The Angel's Injury and a Show of Gratitude

Every day on his way home, Amane passed the park where he and Mahiru had properly met for the first time.

The building where Amane lived was less of a family-use apartment complex and more aimed at single people and couples, so there were few children around, and the surrounding apartment buildings were much the same.

Tucked away and out of sight, the little park close to Amane's building was often deserted. It was in that little park devoid of children, Amane saw Mahiru for the second time.

"What are you doing in a place like this?" he asked.

"…Nothing." Mahiru was sitting on a bench with straight posture and didn't budge at all even after she recognized Amane and looked him over.

In contrast to the first time the two had met there, this time they were already acquainted and were on speaking terms. That had made it easier for Amane to call to Mahiru, but the girl's voice had still been stiff when she answered. It didn't seem like Mahiru was on guard, as she had been during their first encounter. This was something different. Amane could tell that Mahiru was being careful not to let something show on her face.

"Come on, if it was nothing, you wouldn't be sitting here making that face. Did something happen?" Amane inquired.

"…Not really…" Mahiru looked, as she had before when she was on the swing in the rainstorm, like she was lost and didn't know what to do. Seeing her like that worried Amane, but Mahiru didn't seem keen to speak on the matter.

Though he was bound by their tacit promise not to interact outside their apartments, Amane hadn't been able to help calling out to Mahiru when he'd seen her all alone in the park again. Mahiru, for her part, probably did not much want to talk to him; her expression was stiff and blank.

Amane thought it was fine if the girl wasn't feeling up to talking, when he noticed that there were a number of white hairs stuck to her blazer. "You have some hair stuck to your uniform; were you playing with a dog or a cat?" he asked.

"I wasn't playing. I just helped a cat that was stranded up a tree get back down," Mahiru explained.

"What a total cliché… Ah, I get it now."

"Hmm?"

"Wait right there. Don't you dare move."

Amane had finally realized just why Mahiru was sitting there alone on the bench. He sighed and dashed off. He was certain that Mahiru would do as he had asked and would not go anywhere. Actually, it would have been more appropriate to say that she *couldn't* go anywhere.

Muttering to himself about how Mahiru chose the strangest times to act tough, Amane bought a compress and medical tape from the neighborhood drugstore, along with a cup of ice normally used for iced coffee from a convenience store. When Amane at last returned to the park, he found Mahiru sitting on the bench, just as he'd expected. She hadn't so much as shifted.

"Shiina, take off your tights."

"Huh?"

He gave a direct order, and she answered in an extremely cold voice.

"Yeah, I know it's kind of sudden… Look, I'll put my blazer over you and turn around, so take the tights off. We need to ice the injury and put a compress on it."

As expected, Mahiru was none too happy at being ordered to take off her tights, so by way of explanation, Amane waved the bag full of medical supplies.

Mahiru's face understandably tightened. "…How did you know?"

"You had one of your loafers off, and that ankle seemed slightly swollen. Plus, you didn't try to stand up. It really is a total cliché to sprain your ankle while rescuing a cat."

"Oh, be quiet."

"Yeah, yeah. Now, take off your tights and give me your foot."

It was something anyone would have known just from looking, but Mahiru was making a sour face, perhaps because she hadn't expected him to notice that she was hurt. Obediently, Mahiru accepted Amane's blazer and put it over her knees, so it seemed like she was going to listen to what he was saying.

Amane turned his back to Mahiru, put the ice from the cup he had bought at the convenience store into a plastic bag, and poured water over it.

After he tied the top shut so it wouldn't spill out, he wrapped it loosely in a hand towel that he kept in his backpack, making an impromptu ice pack. Then he turned around slowly.

Mahiru had done as he had asked and removed her tights, exposing her bare legs. They were slender and smooth—and looked soft

©SB Creative Corp.

even as she tensed up. The unnatural swelling around her ankle was evident.

"Well, it's not that badly swollen, but it could get worse if you move it too much. First of all, this is going to be cold, but let's ice it for a bit. Once the pain goes away a little, I'll put a compress on, so take it easy," Amane explained.

"…Thank you."

"From now on, just ask for my help. It's not like you'll owe me or anything."

If anything, it's the opposite—I want to pay you back in some small way for everything you've done for me, so I'd appreciate if you would let me solve one or two problems for you.

Mahiru sported her usual expression. Still, she didn't argue with Amane and quietly let him ice her ankle while her leg was propped up on the bench.

"Has the pain gotten any better?" Amane asked after a moment.

"…Yeah, a bit," Mahiru replied.

"All right, I'm putting the compress on, so…don't get mad at me for being a perv or a groper or something, okay?"

"I wouldn't say something so rude to the person helping me."

"Good to hear."

Stressing that he had absolutely no untoward thoughts, Amane squatted down next to Mahiru's leg and stuck a compress on her swollen, red ankle.

When Amane initially asked about the level of pain, it sounded like the sort of thing where Mahiru could still stand and walk, but moving risked agitating the sprain further, so she was better off sitting here quietly. As long as she stayed off it, it would probably remain a minor injury.

Amane had just finished sticking on the compress and was

securing it with medical tape when he noticed Mahiru staring intently down at him.

"You're surprisingly skillful with that," she commented.

"Well, I can do first aid. Still can't cook, though." Amane shrugged, acting a little silly, and Mahiru let out a small laugh. He was glad to see her taut expression relax some, even if it was only a tiny bit. Reassured by Mahiru's slightly softened attitude, Amane pulled the pants of his gym uniform from his backpack.

"Here," he said, handing them to Mahiru.

"What?" she asked.

"Don't make that face at me; I don't like it. Anyway, your legs are exposed, right? And it's not like you can put your tights back on with the compress stuck to you. Relax, I haven't worn them."

It would be bad to let her put her tights back on over her swollen ankle, especially now that it had medical tape wrapped around it. Since it looked so painful, Amane figured Mahiru could wear his gym pants, both as protection from the cold and to stop anyone from seeing her underwear.

Mahiru seemed to understand that he was just trying to be considerate, and so she slipped the pants on.

Amane snatched up his blazer and handed Mahiru the parka he'd been wearing.

"Here, wear this," he told her.

"Wait, but why?"

"Do you want to be seen being carried?"

Letting Mahiru walk on her ankle was a bad idea. Amane had been planning to bring her home from the start. They were both headed to the same place, after all.

"Oh, sorry, but could you put my backpack on?" Amane asked. "I can't carry you on my back if I'm wearing it, obviously."

"Is there an option where you don't carry me?"

"Look here, your ankle is twisted, so you need to rest it. No one's around, and I've got perfectly good legs, so please put them to use."

"Your legs?"

"What, you'd prefer my arms? Would you rather I support you from the side?"

"Are you even strong enough to carry me all that way?"

"Are you making fun of me? …Well, I'm actually not that confident."

Amane knew he could support Mahiru if she leaned on him, but honestly, it would be quite difficult to fully carry her all the way back to the apartment complex. What's more, it would be sure to attract a lot of attention, which Amane preferred to avoid.

He knew that Mahiru had been poking fun when she'd brought up his strength, so he smiled, glad she was feeling well enough to crack jokes like that.

"Look, if you're game, put the hood up and wear my backpack. After you get on my back, take your own bag, too, while you're at it. I won't be able to hold it if I'm supporting you," Amane instructed.

"…Sorry," Mahiru muttered.

"I'm telling you: It's fine. It wouldn't be very manly of me to leave an injured person behind and go home—or to make you walk."

Amane crouched down and turned away from her, and Mahiru timidly leaned onto Amane's back.

Mahiru was wearing Amane's parka, so she had on even more clothes than normal, but even so, he could feel her body pressed against him, slim and willowy.

After confirming that Mahiru's arms were secured around his neck without choking him, Amane stood up slowly, carrying the injured girl on his back.

I knew it; she's so light, Amane thought. He wondered if he should be the one worrying about her diet instead of the other way around. It was more likely that she was just naturally petite, though; that was probably all it was.

Mahiru smelled slightly sweet, and though Amane could tell all sorts of things about how anxious she was feeling based on how tightly she clung to him, he headed for home without showing it.

A few people did stare at the sight of a guy carrying someone on his back, but Mahiru had completely covered her face with the hood of his parka, so Amane wasn't too worried about what little attention was being paid to them.

"All right, here we are." Amane carried Mahiru as far as her front door, then let her down and quickly turned to leave without interfering any further.

Since Mahiru could get around on her own while leaning on a wall, Amane guessed that her injury was probably not all that serious. Thankfully, it was Friday, so Mahiru had plenty of time to rest her ankle and get back on her feet with no problems.

"I don't need dinner tonight, so you should rest. If you like, I could bring you some nutritional supplements," Amane offered.

"I'm fine. I have some stuff prepared," Mahiru answered.

"That's good. See ya."

That was the most important thing: that food wouldn't be a problem. It was essential that Mahiru be able to keep still and rest. Amane watched her open the lock on her front door, and he, too, took out his apartment key.

"...Um," started Mahiru.

"Hmm?"

When Amane heard the girl's voice and turned around, he saw that she was looking up at him timidly, clutching her bag to her chest. She looked somewhat troubled, but as he tilted his head in confusion, she seemed to regain her resolve and looked straight into his eyes.

"…Thank you for what you did today. You really saved me," Mahiru admitted.

"It's fine, really. I just did it because I wanted to. Take care." Embarrassed by the notion of Mahiru fretting over his help, Amane quickly dismissed the thought from his mind. After Mahiru gave him a quick nod, Amane turned to unlock his own door. It was only then that Amane realized that Mahiru was still wearing his parka and athletic pants, but he was sure she would return them another day, so he slipped into his apartment without saying anything.

"Damn, dude, you so healthy that you wear shorts year-round now?"

Amane's melancholy in Monday's gym class had less to do with his lack of athletic talent and more to do with the fact that he was wearing knee-length jersey shorts during an unpleasantly cold season. Everyone else had already switched to their winter gym uniforms, but Amane stood out from all the rest, his legs bare below the knee.

"As if. I just forgot my pants."

"Idiot."

"Shut up."

Amane hadn't seen Mahiru over the weekend, and she still had his gym pants, but he couldn't tell Itsuki that, so there was nothing to do but say that he forgot. He had resigned himself to the inevitable mockery, though when Itsuki slapped his back, cackling with laughter, Amane still found it in himself to slap him back.

Amane let out a soft sigh as he watched Itsuki groan quietly. Then his gaze shifted. At the moment, the boys were practicing their high jumps, and the girls were using the other side of the field. What's more, since two classes of students were using the field at once, it was fairly crowded.

The girls were practicing different track-and-field events, so between taking turns, the girls had plenty of time to watch Amane's class.

"Do your best, Kadowaki!"

Usually, the boys and girls took gym class in different places on campus; with the girls present, the boys were getting all worked up. The girls, on the other hand, all spent their time watching Amane's most popular classmate, the handsome Yuuta Kadowaki.

Amane had never really talked to him before, but he was nice to everyone and was a great student, and on top of that, he was the ace of the track club despite being only a first-year. Everyone knew he was popular with the girls. Amane figured Yuuta must have won some kind of karmic lottery. A lot of the other boys didn't care for him as much, and there were always a lot of sulky looks when he was around.

"Oh wow, looks like Yuuta's as popular as always," Itsuki observed.

"Looks that way," Amane answered dully.

"You don't seem too interested," Itsuki prodded.

"Well, it's not like we're friends or anything; we've barely ever spoken. So why should I care?"

It wasn't as though Yuuta was mean or ever messed with Amane. They had nothing to do with each other, so Amane honestly did not care. He knew that he was in the minority there, but he couldn't bring himself to envy Yuuta the same way all the other boys did. More specifically, Amane knew that Yuuta was so far out of his league that envying him was pointless.

"Typical Amane. What, you don't get jealous now?" Itsuki asked.

"Oh, should I be like 'Wow, I'm sooo jealous of his populaaarity,' huh?" Amane mocked.

"That was pretty good." Itsuki guffawed.

Amane looked over at Yuuta, who was wearing a brilliant smile and basking in feminine adoration. Even Amane had to admit that Yuuta's athletic body and handsome face made him look just like a prince. In fact, some girls had taken to calling him that.

Yuuta rewarded the girls' passionate gazes and shrill voices with another radiant smile and waved back at them. He really knew how to cultivate a following.

"Well, he sure is popular, no arguing with that," admitted Itsuki.

"I know. The other guys can't contain their jealousy," Amane said.

"Ha-ha. But the girls are real energetic, too." Itsuki only had eyes for his girlfriend, Chitose. He had no interest in other girls, so he saw the Yuuta issue as everyone else's problem. Chitose wasn't the least bit interested in Yuuta, so Itsuki probably didn't spend much energy thinking about him.

We've got a prince and an angel... This school has a lot of people with cringey nicknames.

Come to think of it, I wonder if Mahiru the angel ended up getting enough rest. Amane hadn't seen her leave her apartment over the weekend. It was good she was resting comfortably, but he still wondered about the state of her injury.

Amane stealthily scanned the field with his eyes. His class was sharing the field with Mahiru's, so she should've been there. Without too much effort, Amane spotted her. Even in a crowd, the angel was easy to pick out. She hadn't changed into gym clothes and wasn't practicing with the rest of her class. Evidently, she was sitting out today.

Amane was sure that he was not the only boy staring at Mahiru, who sat there looking small and quiet. Though they were far away from each other, their eyes met suddenly, and when Amane shifted his gaze around awkwardly, he saw a small smile pass over Mahiru's lips. Since she was looking toward Amane, that meant she was also looking toward the rest of the boys. Each of Amane's classmates took the smile for their own, nearly inciting a riot.

"Did she just smile at me?!"

"No way; must be me!"

"This is our chance! We've gotta impress her!"

"The prince is hogging the spotlight."

To think that Mahiru could cause such excitement with just one meager smile… Amane didn't know whether it was because she was that amazing or because the boys were all that simple.

"…Buncha morons," Itsuki muttered. He'd apparently been thinking the same thing.

Amane chuckled. "Well, if we don't wanna fail gym class, we'd better get moving, too."

"What's that, Amane? The angel's heavenly gaze got you all riled up, too?"

"No, nothing like that. I told you, I'm not interested."

"Well, guess I'll drop it, then. Since you don't care and all."

Itsuki seemed like he was about to start boasting about how great girlfriends are, likely citing his own personal experience, but Amane was quick to brush him off. "Yeah, yeah," he said. He spared one more glance in Mahiru's direction and smiled wryly.

"Thank you for what you did the other day. Here's your parka and sweatpants back."

That evening, when Mahiru brought him his portion of dinner, she was carrying a paper bag in addition to the plastic container. Amane could see at a glance that the parka and pants he had loaned her a few days ago were folded neatly in the bag.

"Mm. How's the ankle?" he asked.

"The pain is already mostly gone. I've decided not to do any exercise until it's completely healed," Mahiru replied.

"That's for the best. Looks like you're sitting out gym class, too."

"Yeah."

Mahiru had decided to play it safe and not participate in gym, and Amane figured it was probably the right thing to do. Her ankle didn't look like it was hurting her anymore, but she still slightly favored that leg when she walked, indicating that it was not yet entirely healed.

As Amane was nodding at the girl's sensible decision, he thought back on the day's gym class and smiled suddenly. "You know, you're really amazing, Miss Angel. With a single smile, all the boys were practically bursting with excitement."

"I told you to stop calling me that... And it's not as if I like that kind of attention. It really bothers me, you know," Mahiru said.

"Well, who wouldn't get fired up when a beautiful person looks at them? You know, the girls started shrieking today, too, when Kadowaki waved at them."

"...Kadowaki...oh, that super-popular guy?" Mahiru didn't seem to be too interested in the prince. Actually, it seemed like she didn't even recognize his name. Amane had to describe him a bit before Mahiru realized who he was talking about.

Yuuta wasn't as popular as the angel, but he was a fairly well-known boy in their grade, so Amane was surprised that she didn't know who he was.

"You're not interested in him?" Amane asked.

"Not particularly. We're in different classes, and we've never really spoken," Mahiru replied.

"Hmm. The other girls go bananas for him, though. They can't get enough of the cool dude."

"Well, he does have a handsome face. But we don't talk; we don't have any connection. So I don't really care."

"You're so candid about things like that," Amane observed.

"Well, if looks are so important, don't you think it's strange that you don't like me?" asked Mahiru.

"Oh, so you do realize how beautiful you are?"

Mahiru was quite right in what she said. Beauty could be the spark that ignited greater affections, but it was rarely the sole source of love. Amane agreed with that, just as he agreed that Mahiru was very pretty. It was certainly a surprise to hear her say that herself, though.

"I know that, objectively speaking, I'm considered very attractive, and I do work hard to maintain my appearance. It's only natural. Given how often people make a big deal about my looks, I can tell what they think of me even if I don't want to know." Mahiru didn't seem to be boasting in the least.

She was certainly being honest about how much effort she spent on her appearance. Mahiru had always had a good-looking face, but clearly she was not content to coast by on natural good looks. Her hair was like a radiant halo, befitting her angelic nickname, and the luster of her skin was also always perfect, without a single blemish. Her hands didn't get chapped, even when she was doing housework, and even her fingernails were beautifully polished. The gentle curves of her body spoke to a well-balanced figure that had likely taken some effort to cultivate.

"I'm going to say something straight up, so don't get mad at me...," Amane began, "but...you don't seem to be embarrassed by all this praise."

"I'd get annoyed before I'd get embarrassed if someone wouldn't stop flattering me," Mahiru answered curtly.

"Guess being beautiful has its own struggles."

"Still, beauty does have its advantages, so I suppose I shouldn't complain."

"You say that like you wouldn't know..."

"What? Would you rather I bashfully say 'Oh, no, that's not true!'?"

"No, as someone who knows what you're really like, that would be weird."

"Exactly. Honestly, I don't see the point in putting on an act like that in front of you."

"Glad to hear it."

Mahiru had only recently dropped her public persona around Amane, so if she changed back now... Amane could feel goosebumps prickling at the thought of facing the distant angel he saw at school rather than the girl he was gradually getting to know.

In the end, things between the two of them remained as they were.

Amane looked at the food container he'd been handed. There was actually more food than usual. The container was packed with several side dishes, each one a large portion. Rather than leftovers, it was more like Amane had been handed a fancy boxed lunch.

"Today's quite the smorgasbord," he said.

"Because you took such good care of me," Mahiru replied.

"I told you not to worry about that... Oh, there are croquettes in here!" Amane could never say no to croquettes.

Croquettes were frequently sold à la carte but could be a big pain to make yourself. As such, you could consider them the pinnacle of home cooking. After steaming potatoes, mashing them, stirring in sautéed beef, onions, and more, and then forming the patties, you had to completely chill them, then add batter and fry them. It was a very involved process. Even Amane, who rarely cooked anything, had watched his mother make croquettes and had decided never to make them himself because they were such a pain.

"Well, I had them already made and chilling, so I only had to fry them," Mahiru explained.

"Is that why there's fried chicken, too?" asked Amane.

"That's right."

Living alone, Amane didn't get to eat a lot of fried dishes, so he was grateful for the handmade food. Of course, they were best when they were freshly made, while the coating was still nice and crispy, served with hot rice.

"…Sometime, I'd like to try them straight out of the oil," Amane muttered.

Mahiru had packed the fried chicken into the container after letting it cool, perhaps for hygienic reasons. So no matter what, Amane would need to warm the food back up. Though fried foods could be restored to a crispy texture via a toaster oven, it still wasn't the same as eating the stuff fresh. Amane had no doubts that Mahiru's cooking would still be delicious, of course, but it would probably be even better right from the pan.

Amane hadn't meant to whisper what he had been thinking; his desire had simply leaked from his lips. Unfortunately, he'd said it loud enough that Mahiru raised her eyebrows a little.

"Are you inviting me over?" she asked.

"That's not what I'm saying at all! It's already too presumptuous of me to share your meals." Amane hadn't meant it that way at all, and he shrugged and vehemently denied it.

Mahiru brought a hand to her mouth and directed her gaze downward. She seemed to be mulling something over and did not make eye contact with Amane.

"…Your share," she finally said.

"Huh?"

"Let me cook at your place, and we can consider that as part of paying for your share of the food expenses."

Mahiru's sudden proposition left Amane's mouth hanging open in shock.

The accidental mention about eating the fried foods fresh had been more of a sardonic wish than anything else. That Mahiru had actually considered and agreed to it left Amane completely bewildered.

Normally, who would think of going into the home of some boy they didn't know all that well to cook dinner? Maybe it would be more efficient to cook at his place rather than bring the food over after, but he was a member of the opposite sex, and it wasn't like they were close friends. Wouldn't doing that make Mahiru uneasy?

"You definitely don't need to do that; I've already received way more than I could ask for, way more than I deserve... Aren't you worried about your safety?"

"If you try anything, I'll crush you. Hard. No mercy."

"Ack, you're scary! I felt a chill."

"Well, I don't suppose it will come to that. You already know what the risks are, and I've decided you won't do anything. You know how popular I am at school, right?"

"Even supposing I did try something, it'd be the end of me."

Mahiru was vastly more popular than Amane, and on top of that, everyone saw her as this delicate girl, so if word got around that Amane had so much as thought about doing anything inappropriate to her, he was sure he'd never be able to set foot on school grounds again. Amane was not so foolish or so unprincipled as to try something knowing that it would mean, at best, social ruin. He wasn't interested anyway.

"Besides...," Mahiru added.

"Besides?" Amane asked, urging her to continue.

"You're not even the right type for someone like me," Mahiru asserted with a straight face, then suddenly smiled.

"And what if I was your type?" Amane pressed.

"First of all, I believe you were the one who insisted on talking to me. And then wanted nothing to do with me."

"And that won you over?" Amane asked.

"I mean, it told me that you're harmless enough," Mahiru explained.

"Uh, thanks, I guess."

Whether that was a good thing or not, Amane couldn't deny it was true. After all, he had never had any intention of doing anything with Mahiru in the first place. One thing was certain, however: Amane was not going to pass up the chance to enjoy a freshly made meal. He accepted the title of harmless guy and gained the privilege of sharing dinner.

Chapter 8

The First Meal Together

Mahiru was going to start cooking dinner at Amane's apartment, and she presented him with a list of conditions:

- Amane would pay for half the cost of ingredients, plus an additional labor cost, plus the cost of any incidental expenses.
- The two of them would each contact the other no later than the day before if they had something to do and couldn't eat together.
- They would divide the work of shopping and cleaning up afterward.

Regarding the extra labor cost, it had taken some work to get Mahiru to agree to it. Amane had insisted that he felt bad about all the time she was spending on him. It was to be expected, since she did all the work making the food. Aside from that, though, Amane and Mahiru had come to an agreement rather quickly.

And so, the day after their agreement had been ratified, Mahiru came over early holding supermarket bags in both hands and made preparations to start cooking.

"…It's really all brand-new, like it's hardly been used…," Mahiru commented.

"Shut up," Amane shot back.

A beautiful girl stood in his kitchen, and she was wearing an apron. This was like a fantasy come to life. Amane was sure he was going to lose it any second now. When Mahiru pointed out, yet again, that he had really never used his kitchen, he felt a deep shame.

"You've got an impressive collection of gadgets here, but they're like pearls tossed before swine," Mahiru observed.

"Well, if you use them, they won't go to waste," Amane reasoned.

"That's a poor excuse, after the fact. Your precious cookware is practically dying from neglect."

"All right then, bring it back to life with your amazing culinary talents. I sure as hell can't."

With gracious concession, Amane motioned for Mahiru to take over. She returned the gesture with an exasperated expression, but perhaps because she'd expected as much, she just sighed and didn't complain further.

"All right, let's get started. Do you have any spices?"

"Of course I do; are you making fun of me? They're all properly stored—and none are expired, either."

"Wow, I'm surprised."

"It's because they've never been opened."

"That's nothing to brag about. All right, if you don't have what we need, I can bring things over from my place to use this once."

"That would be helpful."

"For now, if you have the basics, I think we can make do. Also, I decided on today's dishes already; is that all right?"

"I don't know much about cooking, so I'm happy with anything as long as I get to eat. I don't have strong preferences."

"Really? Then let's hurry up and get started... Please show me where you keep everything."

"In this basket."

"They're really unopened, huh..."

Mahiru raised her eyebrows in shock as she stared at the basket filled with untouched seasonings. Perhaps because she'd been warned before she'd seen the unused spices, she quickly reassumed her usual demeanor and began washing her hands at the sink.

"All right, I'm going to start making stuff, so you can go wait in the living room or in your bedroom," Mahiru declared.

"Okay. I can't help you with anything anyway," Amane accepted.

"What a gentleman. I suppose you'd just get in the way if you hung around."

"You're awfully honest."

"It's just the truth. There's no need to sugarcoat it."

As Mahiru said, he would clearly just be in the way, so Amane obediently returned to the living room and watched her back as she worked.

When she had finished washing her hands, Mahiru quickly set to work. Amane didn't know what she was making, but based on the ingredients she had readied, it was probably Japanese food.

Everything about this felt strange to Amane, like he was in a dream, but it was real. Mahiru was actually preparing the ingredients right there, her hair tied up in a gently swaying ponytail.

What's with this situation? It's like I've got a wife or something, Amane thought.

Mahiru probably didn't feel the same way, but their setup looked a little too much like they were a happy family, and Amane couldn't help but imagine it. He didn't have even the smallest desire to live with Mahiru, but the sight of a beautiful girl standing in his kitchen was in itself enough to send his mind to all sorts of places. Whether or not there was any affection between Amane and Mahiru, just having a lovely girl treat him to a home-cooked meal was enough to touch Amane's heart.

"...Are you thinking weird things over there?"

"You can stop with the strange speculations."

Amane had frozen when Mahiru called him out. She'd guessed what he was thinking without even turning around.

She sure is sharp...

Feeling amazed and anxious all at once, Amane stamped down on the not-quite-evil base instincts that had begun welling up inside him and returned to staring at Mahiru's back.

About an hour later, Mahiru began setting out completed dishes on the table.

She'd chosen to make Japanese food today, which was typical when one considered her penchant for healthy cooking.

"It turns out you have quite a few utensils and seasonings, so it looks like I won't have to bring anything from my place. Starting tomorrow, I can try more elaborate dishes, too."

"I mean, I'm just grateful you're making anything for me," Amane admitted.

Perhaps because Mahiru hadn't known how many pieces of cookware and seasonings Amane had in his collection, she had made many simple dishes rather than anything more intricate, but the presentation was flawless nonetheless.

Lined up along the table was an array of Japanese-style dishes. From fish simmered in soy sauce to dressed greens. From rolled omelets to miso soup. Every last item was something Amane could never dream of making himself.

Previously, Amane had said he didn't have any particular likes or dislikes, but he did in fact love Japanese food. He wanted to reassure Mahiru, who looked apologetic for having only prepared easy recipes, that this was exactly what he had wanted.

"…It looks amazing," Amane said.

"I'm happy to hear you say that. Eat up while it's still hot."

Mahiru sat down in a chair next to her, so Amane took a seat across the table.

His dining table was small, since he lived alone, so no matter how they sat, they were still close together. It was lucky that Amane happened to have two chairs just in case a guest stopped by, but seeing a beautiful girl sitting right before his eyes evoked some indescribable feeling from within him.

Once Amane set upon the food, however, even Mahiru's beauty ceased to matter.

Hurriedly, he said "Let's eat" and started with the miso soup.

The moment he brought the bowl to his lips and took a sip, the fragrant miso and the flavor of the dashi spread through his mouth. The gentle taste was so completely different from instant miso soup. Amane could tell that it must have been prepared with great care. The miso flavor wasn't overpowering, and it was thoughtfully seasoned to allow the taste of the dashi broth to come through.

At first, Amane felt that the soup's taste was just a little bit strong, but after he considered drinking it while eating the other dishes, he realized that it struck the perfect balance and knew he would empty his bowl. Rather than being overwhelming, the miso soup was a comforting flavor. It was a taste that made you want to eat more.

"Delicious," Amane said with sincerity.

"Thank you for saying so." Mahiru's eyes crinkled in a relieved smile.

Amane had been complimenting Mahiru's cooking for a while,

but she'd probably been feeling nervous with this being the first time she'd cooked right in front of him.

Mahiru watched Amane for a few moments before eating anything herself. Once she finally did start digging in, Amane extended his chopsticks toward the other dishes.

Sampling a bit of each dish, it came as no surprise to Amane that everything Mahiru had prepared was fantastic.

The simmered fish was bursting with juicy flavor without sacrificing its tenderness.

Usually when fish was cooked for a long time to bring out the taste, it would naturally lose some moisture and dry out, but this one was plump and had a nice texture.

As for the rolled omelets, they were tailored exactly to Amane's tastes. They were an enticingly vivid yellow, and when Amane stuffed one in his mouth, he was unsurprised by the gentle seasoning of dashi that greeted him.

When it came to Japanese-style omelets, Amane knew, some people added sugar when making them, while others only used salt. These rolled ones had been flavored with dashi, however. In addition to the rich taste of the dashi, Amane could also taste a faint sweetness. He wondered if that light undertone came from honey. There probably wasn't that much in the rolled omelets, but the satisfying hint of sweetness brought out a real depth.

Amane had no real preference between sweet or salty when it came to egg dishes, but the ones he liked best combined the complex flavor of dashi with what he suspected was a bit of honey. Mahiru had accomplished that expertly, and Amane found himself quite impressed.

Quietly muttering that the rolled omelets were delicious, Amane grabbed another one with his chopsticks and quickly tossed it in his mouth.

Not only had they been perfectly flavored, they'd been skillfully cooked as well. The stock added to the eggs made them extra juicy.

These are definitely better than Mom's rolled omelets. He kept rude thoughts about his nonpresent mother to himself as he smacked his lips happily. Then he realized that Mahiru was staring at him.

"...You really seem to be enjoying it."

"Because it's all so good. I'm paying my respects to the delicious food."

"Sure, all right."

"Besides, doesn't it feel better when I'm honest about how much I enjoy it rather than sitting here eating with a blank expression?"

If you think something's delicious, you've got to really act like it, otherwise, the person who made it will be left wondering. Even if you say you enjoy it, who would believe you if you didn't look the part? It's better to be honest and just let how you feel show directly on your face. Whether you're the one giving thanks or being thanked, it's best to do what feels good.

"...Yes, I suppose so..." Mahiru seemed to understand what Amane was saying, and she smiled slightly. It was a gentle expression, and it betrayed just a hint of relief. It was sweet enough that all of Amane's thoughts ground to a halt for a second.

"...Fujimiya?" Mahiru asked.

"Ah...no, it's nothing," Amane replied. He'd been enchanted by the angel's smile, but he couldn't possibly tell her that. To conceal his growing embarrassment, Amane took another bite of food, ending any further discussion.

"...Thank you for dinner."

"I'm glad you liked it."

Amane had completely devoured every dish Mahiru had laid out. Mahiru's words had been calm, but her expression was serene, and she seemed happy that Amane had packed everything into his stomach. Not a single grain of rice had been left behind.

"It was delicious," Amane complimented.

"I could tell that much just by watching you," Mahiru quipped dryly.

"Better than my mom's cooking."

"I hear it's taboo to compare a girl's cooking to your mother's."

"Isn't that only true when you're criticizing someone? Anyway, does that bother you?"

"I don't mind, no."

"Well then, it's fine, right? It doesn't change the fact that it's delicious."

Mahiru was clearly no amateur cook. Amane's mother probably had more years of experience under her belt, but she preferred different tastes, and many of her dishes were fairly bland, so they were no match for Mahiru's carefully concocted foods.

"...Man, this is so awesome. To be able to eat like that every night!" exclaimed Amane.

"As long as I don't have anything else going on, that is," Mahiru added.

"...So I can really host you every night for dinner?"

"I wouldn't have suggested it if I was against the idea."

"Well, I guess that's true."

Mahiru was a straight shooter, so of course she would've never agreed to it if she didn't want to in the first place. Amane still wasn't sure if it was okay to have her cooking for him like this so often, however.

He was paying for half the ingredients, plus a bit extra to cover her labor, but even so, he couldn't help feeling like the burden on Mahiru was too large.

"...Do you normally cook for boys you don't even like?" Amane asked.

"I'm doing it because you were neglecting your health. Besides, I enjoy the act of cooking itself, and I don't hate seeing you eat it with such gusto."

"But...," Amane started.

"If it bothers you that much, it would be no problem to stop."

"No, please, I'm begging you."

At the first sign of Mahiru possibly not cooking for him anymore, Amane instantly retracted any and all complaints. That was just how much her food meant to him. To have it snatched away now—it would practically be a matter of life and death.

Amane was entirely aware that Mahiru had gained full control of him by way of his stomach, but Mahiru's cooking was just too delicious to refuse. Returning to convenience-store meals now would be like robbing the world of color.

Shocked at Amane's immediate reply, Mahiru was stunned for a moment before breaking into a smile.

"Well then, please continue to enjoy."

"...Okay."

It appeared that Amane's days of dining with the extremely charitable angel who made all the food by hand would continue for a while yet. Amane couldn't help but sigh from happiness, guilt, and anticipation.

Chapter 9

The Angel's Birthday

"Amaneee, how'd you do?"

Semester exams had finally ended. Having survived their collective hell, the students gathered in their classroom, more exited and animated than usual.

Amane and Itsuki, both relieved that they had wrapped up all their tests, were comparing their performances.

"Mm? Oh, pretty average," Amane answered. "Not that great, not that bad."

The exam had covered the expected material, so for anyone who studied daily, it wasn't that difficult. Amane had done about as well this time as he had with other tests, leaving little to say about his academics one way or the other.

Amane got bored easily, but he nevertheless always made sure to study. He was able to retain most of the things taught in class, but it was far too difficult to get a perfect score, so his scores usually floated between a solid eighty and ninety.

"I bet you'll make it into the top thirty, if you didn't outdo yourself...you egghead," Itsuki teased.

"It's because I study every day," Amane shot back.

"Well, how nice for you!"

"Don't start; you're the one forgetting to study 'cause you're too busy flirting."

The difference between Amane and Itsuki probably had less to do with their intellectual capacities and more to do with which one of them spent all their free time with a certain girlfriend named Chitose. Itsuki had the ability to make it into a pretty high score bracket if he ever bothered to study seriously, but since Chitose was his real priority, his actual rank was much lower than Amane's.

"…Girlfriends are great, you know?" Itsuki said wistfully.

"Yeah, yeah."

"Hey, Amane, you should get a girlfriend, too!"

"If guys could just get girlfriends whenever they wanted, the men of the world wouldn't shed so many bitter tears."

There were plenty of unsatisfied men who would have taken offense at Itsuki's thoughtless remark. Amane, though, wasn't really inclined to get angry with him over it. In fact, he'd never really felt that way about any girl, so he was content to let the comment pass.

"Assuming I did get one, what then?" Amane inquired.

"A double date," Itsuki replied.

"That would end in a bad case of heartburn for my fictional girlfriend and me. We'd have to break up."

"You could flirt in front of us, too, y'know!"

"Do you really think I can find a girlfriend, the way I live?"

"…I guess it's impossible."

"Right?"

Amane was honest to a fault, even with himself. He'd always found other people difficult and exhausting, and he was aware that many people found him to be standoffish. That, plus the blunt way he spoke, meant he was not all that popular. Amane's social status would've made it hard to find a girlfriend, even if he was looking for one.

Against all odds, if Amane did somehow find a girlfriend, he was sure they wouldn't be like Itsuki and Chitose. He couldn't picture himself flirting in public with a girl, oblivious to anyone who might see.

"Come on, you should at least find someone you like, Amane. If you just cut your bangs a little shorter, cleaned yourself up, and maybe found a style that worked for you, the girls would definitely look at you differently, I'm tellin' ya."

Assuming Amane's self-evaluation was accurate, he didn't have the handsome looks of a pretty boy like Yuuta or a Romeo like Itsuki, but he definitely didn't think he was ugly, either. Amane figured that if he just spent more time on his grooming and paid more attention to his clothes, he could rival most of the other boys his age. The problem was that he didn't know enough about fashion to dress well, and he was certainly not smooth enough with his words to win any girl over.

"I'm not interested in the kind of girl who picks a date based on appearance," Amane asserted.

"You say that, but if you don't get them interested in the first place, you won't even get to know them well enough to judge their personality, right?" Itsuki argued back.

"…Even if that's true, I'm not really looking for a girlfriend right now."

Were some hypothetical girl ever actually interested in Amane, it would be all over the second she saw how he lived. Amane was a slob with no life skills, and on top of that, he had a difficult time getting along with other people. If there was a girl who was drawn to him, despite all that, he'd like to meet her. Such a hopeless thought was enough to bring a bitter smile to Amane's face.

Besides, since Mahiru was cooking dinners for him now, a girl-friend could introduce some unpleasant complications. Not that Amane intended to pursue a relationship in the first place, but that was simply one more strike against the idea.

Amane felt that Mahiru's delicious cooking was worth more than the possibility of an as-yet-unseen girlfriend, and that conviction was not likely to be easily overturned.

"Ugh, you're so boring... How about I get Chi to introduce you to one of her friends?" offered Itsuki.

"You care way too much about this. Most of Chi's friends are too...excitable. It's hard for me to hang out with them, even as friends." Amane quickly shot down the idea.

"Only because you're so gloomy."

"Oh, shut up."

"Well, if you say so, I won't say anything to her for now. But as a blossoming high school boy, isn't it sad to live an empty life, all by yourself?"

"I don't need a girlfriend; they're too much trouble."

Just what do you think we're supposed to be doing at school any-way? Amane thought. Even if he wasn't actually that serious about his studies, he still didn't see the point in spending so much time worrying about romance. Above all, finding a real match was no easy feat.

"...What a waste," Itsuki grumbled.

"Yeah, yeah." Amane shrugged.

"But listen, you'll change your tune when you find a good one, Amane, ya hear?"

"What makes you so sure?"

"Because girls particularly like to fuss over guys like you."

"Whatever you say, man."

Amane couldn't imagine acting so sentimental; it didn't seem possible. He decided to simply ignore his friend's words. Itsuki was looking at Amane with an exasperated glare, when suddenly, his line of sight shifted, and his face relaxed.

"Itsukiii! Let's go home together!"

"Ah, Chi!"

Just then, Chitose appeared. Apparently, Itsuki had promised to walk her home, which brought a swift end to their conversation.

When Amane turned to see where his friend's attention had shifted, he saw a girl with medium-short light-brown hair tinged with red, looking their way with a radiant smile. Well, to be more accurate, she was only looking and waving at Itsuki.

The girl's lively aura and bright, smiling face were enough to make Itsuki beam whenever he saw her. That was the kind of effect Chitose had on people, and for better or worse, she was always the center of attention.

Chitose was a different type of beauty than Mahiru. She had a great big smile as she rushed over. With any luck, she wouldn't have much to say today, because usually whenever Chitose talked, she made fun of Amane.

"You agree, right, Chi? Amane's the type of guy who needs a girl-friend to take care of him, don't you think?" Itsuki asked.

"Don't stick your nose where it doesn't belong," chided Amane.

"Wait, what, do you have a girlfriend, Amane?!" Chitose exclaimed excitedly.

"No way."

"Aw, bummer," Chitose said, pouting. "If you did, I'd want to be friends with her."

"Knowing your idea of friendship, I would feel bad for my imag-inary girlfriend," Amane said.

"Oh, so you have an *imaginary* girlfriend?" Chitose asked.

"Weren't we just talking about *what if* I had one?!"

"Kidding, kidding."

"I get tired just talking to you…"

"That's just because you don't have the stamina to handle me."

"Don't have the patience, more like…"

Even a short exchange with Chitose was mentally exhausting for Amane. Most of the time, he tried to keep his head down and avoid other people, like at school. When he found himself forced to carry on a conversation with someone as extroverted as Chitose, it was really demanding.

Chitose didn't let Amane's sour attitude bother her at all and flashed the exhausted-looking boy a truly joyful-looking smile. "You're such a mess."

Itsuki smiled in the same way and tossed out some perfunctory advice. "You'd better get your act together, buddy."

Amane was already too worn-out, managing only to let out a deep sigh.

"…What are you doing?"

After returning home and gobbling up Mahiru's handmade food, Amane returned to the living room once he was finished doing the dishes and saw Mahiru with a question sheet spread out before her.

There'd been no agreement about cleaning the dishes, but Amane took the initiative to shoulder the burden whenever possible. While he'd been tidying up, Mahiru had gone to sit in the living room. It would have been inexcusable to make her do everything and then hurry on home.

"I'm grading," Mahiru answered.

"I mean, I can see that."

She seemed to be reviewing her answers with her textbook out, checking that she hadn't gotten anything wrong.

"So what's the result?" Amane asked.

"Well, if I didn't make any recording errors on my answer sheet, then it's…a perfect score."

"I can't think of anything to say except 'It figures.'"

Just as Mahiru didn't show much of a reaction in regard to her errorless work, Amane didn't have a very exaggerated response. He wasn't surprised, because her name was practically always written in the top spot of the periodic exam results. He knew Mahiru was more than capable of a perfect score, so he was not the least bit surprised by her performance here.

"It's because studying doesn't bother me. I've actually already completed all of this year's coursework, so now it's enough to simply review," Mahiru explained.

"Whoa, you really go all out…," Amane replied.

"You study a lot yourself, Fujimiya."

"You know what my grades are like?"

"I sort of remember your name in the ranking list."

Apparently, Mahiru had known a little bit about Amane before they ever spoke. She must have noticed him among the top ranks, because she recounted his exact placement on the most recent test without hesitation, almost like she was looking at the list right now.

Amane did work pretty hard at his studies, but it wasn't because of some earnest drive for success or anything. It was because of an agreement he'd come to with his parents. In order to live alone, he had to maintain good grades.

"Well, it's a condition for my current lifestyle: I have to keep my grades up."

The only other facet to the agreement was that Amane had to visit home at least once every six months, but he could take care of that over long school breaks. Basically, as long as he was keeping his grades up, there were no problems.

"I study hard enough to keep my head above water, but nothing like you. You really put a lot of effort in."

"…I have to try hard," Mahiru mumbled, casting her eyes downward. Her expression was hidden by her bangs, and while Amane couldn't get a proper look at it, anyone would have recognized it wasn't a happy one. Before he could get a read on her, though, she quickly looked back up, once again wearing her usual expression.

Even if there had been time to point out the curious change, Amane probably wouldn't have. He could tell that Mahiru was carrying some kind of painful burden by certain things she did or faces she made.

While Amane made sure to never ask Mahiru what was bothering her or what was so unpleasant, he still got the impression that she was struggling with something. Amane imagined that, whatever it was, it had its origins in her home life. It was hardly the kind of subject he could just casually broach with the girl. He understood that this was not an area in which an outsider like himself could intrude, and so Amane never touched the subject, and he persistently tried to maintain a sense of distance appropriate for a neighbor.

Everyone had things they didn't want to talk about, even Amane. Treading thoughtlessly on Mahiru would be rude, and he was sure that she appreciated the fact that he pretended not to notice her distress.

Having disguised her abrupt change in mood, Mahiru declared in a clear voice that she would be heading back to her own apartment. She put her textbook and her answer sheet back into her bag.

Amane didn't have any intention of stopping her, so he replied simply "Mm-hmm, sounds good" and watched Mahiru get ready to leave.

When the angel had finished putting everything away, she stood up from her seat, and Amane noticed that she'd left something behind next to her empty cup. He picked it up and discovered it was a case holding Mahiru's student ID, the kind any student would have. She'd probably pulled it out along with her textbook and forgotten to put it away.

Along with her name and picture, the little plastic card displayed common information, like her student number, birthday, and blood type. After staring at it for a second, Amane called out to Mahiru, who was in the entryway and putting her shoes on.

"You forgot this," he said.

"Oh, sorry for the trouble. Well then, good night."

"Night."

Mahiru gave a quick, polite bow and turned her back on Amane's apartment. With a small sigh, Amane watched her leave.

Thinking back to the birth date listed on Mahiru's school ID, Amane put a hand to his forehead as he realized something.

"…That's in four days, isn't it?"

If he hadn't unintentionally seen the girl's ID, he likely never would've found out. Amane wished that he'd known about Mahiru's birthday a little earlier and let out another sigh, a deep one.

"Hey, I was wondering, is there anything you want?"

The following day, Amane tried to see if there was anything Mahiru might like as a gift.

There was no ulterior motive behind the gesture. In fact, Amane had been thinking for a while that it might be nice to get something for the girl who had been taking care of him every day. A birthday seemed like the perfect time.

There must have been something odd about the way Amane phrased the question, however, because Mahiru gave him a puzzled look. One that made Amane begin to regret asking such a direct question.

"Why are you asking all of the sudden?" Mahiru inquired.

"You don't seem very materialistic, so I was just curious."

"Out of nowhere again…"

Amane thought that he should probably have tried to play it a little smoother, but it was too late for that now. The one possible saving grace was that Mahiru didn't seem to have realized that this was about her birthday. As far as she knew, Amane should've had no way of knowing her date of birth. Hopefully, that would keep her from catching on.

"Well, let's see, there is one thing I need. I guess that's what I want right now."

"What do you want?"

"A whetstone."

"A…whetstone?"

Unconsciously, Amane repeated Mahiru's words, because the girl's answer had been far too unexpected.

No one could've expected that kind of answer from a high school girl. Normally, you'd think they would want cosmetics, or accessories, or bags, or something like that, Amane thought. He would never in his wildest dreams have expected a girl to want a tool for sharpening metal.

"That's right, a whetstone. I already have several, but I want one with a finer finishing surface, you see," Mahiru explained.

"Are you sure you're really an ordinary high school girl?" Amane asked.

"Please don't expect me to be ordinary."

It was difficult for Amane to object to that. Mahiru could not be called an ordinary high schooler, by any standard. Describing her as an angel seemed entirely accurate. Mahiru was a prodigy who was good at school and sports. What's more, she was an excellent cook and a skilled housekeeper. As if that wasn't enough, Mahiru was a noble young lady who spent so much time taking care of a slob like Amane that she could've been mistaken for a married woman.

Still, who could have imagined she'd want something like a whetstone?

Mahiru had to be the only high school girl in the whole world who wanted such a thing.

"You can't buy it yourself?" Amane wondered aloud. She was well-off, after all.

"It's not exactly that I can't buy it, you know. It's just—I won't have that many opportunities to use it, and it's pretty expensive. After considering all that, I couldn't really justify the purchase. I already have one that can put a decent edge on, so I keep telling myself that I don't really need it."

Amane had to admit that it was more than a bit frightening to know that Mahiru owned several whetstones already.

"...How many high school girls out there sharpen their own kitchen knives?" he asked.

"Quite a few," Mahiru replied.

"Even if there are, you're the only one I know, and you're also the only one who wants another whetstone."

"Well, I suppose it's nice to be unique."

"If you say so..."

This certainly was an angel with unusual interests. Amane couldn't make heads or tails of her.

Mahiru tilted her head in confusion as Amane stood there looking baffled. He'd completely lost sight of his original objective.

"Hey, Itsuki?"

After completely failing to decide on a gift that Mahiru might appreciate, Amane had decided instead to consult with his best friend.

Itsuki had a way with women's hearts, as well as a girlfriend to consult, so Amane expected that he would probably have some grasp on what a girl would normally want. While he wasn't really sure it was a good idea to try to apply normal standards to someone like Mahiru, he expected that she wouldn't outright hate things that made someone else's girlfriend happy.

"What's up?" Itsuki replied.

"When you give Chitose presents, what do you usually get her?"

Amane thought it would be best to start by asking what Itsuki bought for his girl, but all he got back was a blank stare.

"Huh, you planning on giving a present to some sweetheart of yours?"

"Do you think I have it in me to do something like that?"

"Nope."

"All right, then."

"In that case, why are you asking?"

"Someone I know has a birthday coming up, so I wanted to ask you."

While Amane was planning on listening to Itsuki's advice with the utmost attention, he was also keen not to reveal too much about his own circumstances.

"Hmm...for starters, you should try finding out what they want. You know, it's important to do that sort of research on a regular basis. It's the secret to a harmonious relationship, I'm telling you," said Itsuki.

"I told you that this isn't for a girlfriend," Amane reminded.

Setting aside the potential grave danger the other boys at school would pose to Amane's physical safety if word ever got around, Mahiru was too awe-inspiring to even consider asking out in the first place.

Sure, he was comfortable hanging around with her, and they got along well enough as two frank individuals, but there were absolutely no romantic feelings between them. Sure, she was cute, but that didn't mean Amane wanted a relationship.

"What they want, huh...? And what if you don't know?" Amane asked.

"Depends on how close you are. If you're good friends, an accessory or something is good, but if you're not close, something practical that they can use is a safer bet. There are lots of girls who're happy to get flowers but don't know what to do when they receive them," Itsuki explained.

"...You sure know your stuff."

"Well, I've done a fair bit of research, I guess."

Itsuki and Chitose hadn't always been so wild about each other. Their relationship had slowly developed, first starting in middle school. Amane had gone to a different middle school, so he didn't really know all the details, but apparently, they'd gone through a lot together, and their relationship had grown from those experiences to the point where these days, they wouldn't shut up about each other.

To hear him tell it, Itsuki had also been fairly lost the first time he'd had to give Chitose a present, so Amane figured he could benefit from his friend's experience.

"Oh, and no girl hates hand cream," Itsuki added.

"Hand cream?"

As Amane was pondering this unexpected option, Itsuki grinned and explained proudly, "No matter what age they are, every girl has some use for it. If she's a student, her hands get dry from handling notebooks and textbooks in class; if she's in the workforce, her hands dry out from typing and air conditioning; and housewives cook and clean, so their hands take a beating, too. You can't go wrong with that stuff."

"Hmm. You sure know an awful lot about women's hands...," Amane said.

"You're the one who came and asked me!" Itsuki snapped.

Itsuki slapped Amane on the back, but there was no power behind it. The two friends shared a laugh.

Hand cream, huh? I guess that is a pretty safe bet.

Amane had been taking the initiative on washing the dishes after dinner, but Mahiru obviously did her own dishes at home, so he could imagine her hands could use some moisturizing. More importantly, Amane was sure she took care of her hands already, since they were so smooth. A gift she could use right away really was the best plan.

"Cool, thanks for your thoughts," Amane said.

"Let's try asking Chi, too. As a fellow girl, she probably has a better idea," proposed Itsuki.

"...Eh..."

"You gotta warm up to her."

Amane certainly didn't hate her, but Chitose was not exactly his favorite type of girl, and being around her always made him feel awkward. Usually, he tried to avoid interacting with her altogether. Itsuki slapped Amane's back again gently, smiling in amusement.

"Whaaa—? Amane, you're giving a girl a birthday present?" Chitose was smiling—no, smirking—at this rare development, and it was all Amane could do not to grimace.

He had gone to Chitose's classroom to talk to her after school, and sure enough, she seemed greatly amused. Incidentally, Itsuki had sent Chitose a message saying that he wasn't worried about her being alone with another boy as long as it was Amane, so he had gone on home. Amane had sighed softly, while Chitose had worn a wide grin.

I told him I didn't want to ask her.

It was obvious that she was definitely going to pry and ridicule him, so he hadn't intended to turn to her for help at all. Amane certainly didn't hate Chitose, but he couldn't deny that there were some things about her that he just couldn't stand.

"Okay, so Itsuki wrote here that *'Amane was hoping you'd give him some pointers.'* So you want my help, huh?"

"You're the only girl I can ask, Chi."

"It doesn't sound very nice when you put it like that, you know." Chitose looked at Amane with clear pity, but he let it pass.

The truth was, Amane had no female friends outside of Chitose. Every single girl in his class barely counted as acquaintances, and he wasn't close enough to any of them to be able to ask for help with things like this.

Actually, Amane was usually rather quiet in school. If one of his female classmates tried to talk to him, he probably wouldn't know what to do.

"All right, well, I can't imagine you really understand how girls think, Amane. But don't worry! Miss Chitose is here to advise you!"

"…I guess I'm in your hands," Amane said.

"You guess? What's to guess? I may not look it, but I know women's hearts perfectly!"

"I mean, you are a girl, after all…I guess."

"Watch it with those guesses, buddy! I'm not sure I like what you're implying!"

Chitose cleared her throat and thrust out her chest. Compared to Mahiru, who Amane saw every day, the result was underwhelming at best. Amane awkwardly stared at the ground.

Regardless of what he personally thought, Chitose was popular with guys. Personality-wise, she was cheerful and friendly, and she talked to everyone without playing favorites, so hers was a different kind of popularity than Mahiru's. She got along with boys and girls alike. She really was the epitome of a life-of-the-party kind of person.

She had apparently been a member of the track-and-field club in middle school, and her slender build and toned legs certainly didn't hurt her popularity. It was a verifiable fact that her legs were beautiful, so much so that Itsuki had warned other guys in school that he'd get angry if they stared at her too much.

"Ah, right, right," Chitose chittered. "Something for a cute girl, let's see…"

There were definitely times when she got too friendly, but Amane wouldn't deny that Chitose was cute. He could understand why other guys in school liked her.

"…You know," Chitose added, "that glum attitude of yours is seriously gonna give people the wrong idea."

"Gee, thanks for your concern," Amane replied.

"Fine, fine. So you're giving something to a girl, right? Well, what kind of girl?"

Chitose's question didn't leave him much room to maneuver, but Amane knew that if he was careless with what he told her, she wouldn't let him live it down, so he chose his words gingerly.

"She's an acquaintance of mine, and she's relatively young. Beyond that, I'm exercising my right to remain silent."

"Uh…if you won't tell me her about her personality or what she likes, even I can't come up with any ideas, you know."

"Can't you just tell me some things that you would like to get as a gift? Then I'll choose from among them."

"I get it; you don't want to tell me anything about her. Fine, we'll do it your way."

Chitose made a good point, but if he told her any more, she would know that Amane was close to a girl their age, and it was likely that the conversation would veer off in a strange and uncomfortable direction from there. If he really slipped up, Chitose might even end up figuring out that he was talking about Mahiru.

Amane wanted to avoid that if at all possible, so he'd decided not to tell her anything that wasn't strictly necessary. Chitose also seemed to understand that he wouldn't willingly reveal much more, and thankfully, she was kind enough to back off on the questions.

"Hmm, let's see… I don't know what type of relationship you have with her, but if she's an acquaintance you speak with fairly often, I'm assuming she would be happy to receive something from a person who's about as close to her as I am to you. In that case, generally a consumable or everyday item that's not too expensive should be good."

"Itsuki told me pretty much the same thing," Amane said.

"Obviously. He understands how girls think. Now, if you're looking for a casual gift, some sweets and a handkerchief or some small item might be good. If I got an expensive accessory from you, Amane, I'd totally be like 'A bribe?!' or something."

"I don't think I would get anything out of bribing you, though."

After shooting Amane a glance that seemed to be asking for some sort of recompense for her help, Chitose smiled and answered, "Well, you've got that right. Anyway, little things like that are safe."

"…Gotcha."

"You sound kinda unsatisfied." Chitose cocked her head.

"It's not that I'm not satisfied, but…" Amane trailed off. In truth, he just wasn't sure that Mahiru would appreciate the sort of gift that he would select. She probably had impeccable taste, and she seemed like the type to choose things that combined quality and functionality. Amane wasn't sure if his choice would measure up.

Chitose could sense a slight hesitation in Amane's demeanor, and she hummed a bit to herself. "…Let's see… Another option might be…something cute?"

"…Such as?"

"Depends on the person's tastes. For example, a stuffed animal or a keychain with an adorable character on it. I think giving her something like that might work."

Amane blinked back at Chitose after hearing the unexpected suggestion, and Chitose smiled knowingly. "Most girls enjoy cute things, you see. There are even some people who keep collecting stuffed animals long after they grow up, and lots of girls like them in general, right?"

"...A stuffed animal, huh...?" Amane didn't know whether Mahiru had any girly interests, but she did wear clothes decorated with cute frills and ornaments, so she probably didn't hate cuter things like stuffed animals.

Amane could certainly imagine Mahiru being happy to receive a plush toy.

"Oh, do I sense some interest?" Chitose smirked. Apparently, she had caught the minute change that had come over Amane. He nodded, though he was still unsure, and let out a small sigh.

"...But it'll be too weird for me to buy a stuffed animal, I think," Amane admitted.

"It's a present; you're not buying it for yourself. What's the problem?" Chitose asked.

"I mean, a guy my age, carrying a stuffed animal to the register...?"

"You really are pathetic, you know that?"

"Mm-hmm."

There was no denying it, but it still hurt Amane to hear it. He ought to be able to get over such a petty hang-up, but even walking into a store that carried stuffed animals by himself was enough to make him feel embarrassed.

Fortunately, Chitose was with him today. Amane thought he might be able to convince her to accompany him to a shop on the way home. It certainly wasn't out of the question, but...

"...Chitose, come with me," said Amane.

"Whatcha mean?"

"...Please accompany me to go shopping."

"Hmm, I wonder if I should..." It was just like Chitose to tease him like this.

Of course, she didn't really have any intention of refusing Amane's request, but there could be no doubt that she was putting on a deliberate act, both to make fun of Amane and to force him to beg for her help.

"I'm asking you, please. I'm really counting on you," Amane pleaded.

"Mmm, I guess I could go... By the way, Amane, I feel like eating something sweet. And the crepe stand in front of the station has a super-delicious-looking limited-time item..."

"...Please allow me to treat you."

"Yay!"

Amane grimaced at Chitose's clever manipulation, but he realized it was a small price to pay for her help. It was way better to pay for one crepe than to go into a cutesy shop all on his own. Amane let out a powerful sigh as he looked at Chitose, who was grinning impishly, then mentally calculated his approximate budget based on what was in his wallet.

After consulting Itsuki and Chitose, Amane had at last made a decision on what to give Mahiru for her birthday. Staring at the back of the girl in question, a nervous expression overtook Amane's face.

As compensation for a deluxe crepe from the shop in front of the station, the Wintertime Limited Edition Berry Berry Special to be exact, Amane had asked Chitose for one more thing. It and the actual present were now sitting in a bag together. The problem was that Amane was completely at a loss for when he should give the gift to Mahiru.

The birthday girl was fixing dinner as usual, with no change in demeanor.

Amane didn't know what was on the menu, but it had the air of Japanese food and certainly didn't seem like anything special. She seemed relaxed as she went about her preparations.

Mahiru had made no indication at all that today was anything but another regular day. She was acting so normal that Amane wondered if perhaps she even knew.

As Mahiru started setting the table, Amane couldn't help but notice that her face remained completely unchanged. The two ate an extremely typical dinner and held a totally normal conversation. Through it all, Amane remained completely unsure of when best to present her with the gifts he'd gotten. Frowning, he glanced in the direction of the paper bag hidden behind his sofa.

He decided to wait until they had cleaned up after dinner and returned to the living room, when he could take a seat beside Mahiru on his two-person sofa. She'd brought some books to look over after their meal, so that seemed as good a time as any.

True to her nickname, the angel was just as beautiful when she was reading.

Without knowing why, Amane hesitated a little to sit next to her, but even if he hesitated, there was no way around it, so he grabbed the paper gift bag from its hiding place and sat down next to Mahiru.

Immediately, the girl's head snapped up. Whether she'd noticed Amane's presence or heard the sound of the crinkling paper bag was unclear. Either way, her caramel-colored eyes turned toward Amane before shifting to what he was holding.

Mahiru looked confused, as if she still hadn't realized that this was about her birthday.

"Here. For you." Amane placed the bag on Mahiru's knees, and the girl's expression grew even more puzzled.

"What is this?" she asked.

"It's your birthday, right?"

"That's true…but wait, how did you know that? I don't remember telling anyone." Mahiru was suddenly on guard.

"Remember when you dropped your school ID in my apartment?" Amane reminded her.

She seemed to understand, and her normal expression returned. "I really wish you hadn't gone to the trouble. I…don't celebrate my birthday."

Amane was certain that he'd heard a bit of cold detachment in Mahiru's voice when she spoke. The look in her eyes told him that even the word *birthday* was something she avoided.

I see, he thought. *So the reason why she didn't act any differently, even though it's her birthday, wasn't because she forgot… She's been purposely ignoring it. Something about it must bother her.*

Amane figured that if that wasn't the case, Mahiru wouldn't have spoken like that.

"Okay then, call it an expression of gratitude for everything you do for me. I just decided to give you something to repay you."

Setting aside any mention of Mahiru's birthday, Amane pressed the bag on her, justifying it as his way of thanking her for her daily kindnesses. She cooked delicious meals for him every evening and helped him with his cleaning sometimes. When it came down to it, Mahiru did a lot to take care of Amane. He wanted to repay that debt in whatever small way possible.

Amane held out the present to Mahiru, but she shrank away. First, she looked confused, then she frowned at Amane's determination. Finally, she accepted the gift bag.

"…Well, can I open it?" Mahiru asked.

"Yeah," Amane said.

Mahiru nodded and gingerly pulled out the box that was inside the paper bag, then she carefully untied the ribbon and removed the wrapping paper.

Something about watching Mahiru open the gift made Amane extremely nervous.

Inside the box was the hand cream Itsuki had suggested. It was nestled in a largish box alongside some sweets. Apparently, it'd been some kind of set. It wasn't the kind of hand cream that smelled particularly nice, nor was it all that stylish. Instead, it was the scentless kind that was gentle on the skin. That way, it wouldn't cause any trouble while doing housework. This was the sort that was advertised as moisture-retaining. Amane had made sure to check the reviews of the product on the Internet, so he was certain of its efficacy.

"Yeah, sorry it's nothing too crazy. I just thought that since you do a lot of housework, your hands might get dry. They had scented ones, too, but I thought you might have some of those already. Apparently, it's effective and easy on the skin."

"It is…quite practical," Mahiru said.

"I thought you would value practicality over anything else," answered Amane.

"Yeah, you're right. Thank you very much." Mahiru smiled slightly, as if she understood Amane's reasoning. A little less nervous now, Amane's expression softened a bit as well. It seemed like he'd made a good impression.

There was one more present, though, and Amane felt embarrassed to have Mahiru open this one in front of him for some reason. He'd hoped that she would only notice it after she had gone back home.

However, Mahiru was peering into the paper bag, looking as if she had already noticed that there was one more thing hiding within it.

"…What, a second one?" she asked.

"Ah. Yeah, there is. It's a bonus; I picked it out myself," Amane answered.

"What does that mean?"

"…Exactly what I said."

Amane averted his eyes. Mahiru tilted her head in confusion for an instant, then promptly pulled the second gift from the bag.

To purposefully disguise this other present, Amane had intentionally wrapped it in paper the same color as the interior of the bag. He'd hoped that would make it stand out less—and that Mahiru would only notice it later when he wasn't around. Unfortunately, it was large enough that Amane should've known it would be impossible to miss. There was honestly no way Mahiru could have overlooked it.

Unlike the hand cream, this present didn't come in a box, just a polyester bag. It was just about the right size to fit comfortably in Mahiru's arms. The bag was tied up with a navy-blue ribbon, and Amane watched Mahiru undo that carefully as well, wondering if it would be all right for him to stand up from his seat. Finally, Mahiru carefully pulled out what lay inside.

She held the bag's contents up gently with both hands, blinking her large eyes dramatically, looking truly surprised.

"…A bear?" Mahiru mumbled.

It was a stuffed animal. Not too large, it was perfectly proportioned for an elementary school student. Its light-colored fur was soft, much like Mahiru's own hair. A light-blue ribbon was tied around the toy's neck to form a collar. It had a rather cherubic look stitched onto its face, and the round, cute button eyes had a luster to them that reflected Mahiru's face as they stared at her.

Doubtless, the girl was wondering why Amane had given her such a thing when she was in high school. The truth was that Amane had taken a risk and chosen it based on Chitose's advice that girls liked cute things no matter how old they were.

Of course, he had been much too embarrassed to go buy the bear alone, so Chitose had come with him to make the purchase, though only in exchange for the deluxe crepe from the shop in front of the station.

Chitose's smiling face had loomed over Amane throughout the whole process of buying the bear and getting it wrapped. In the end, he couldn't help but think it might've been better if he'd just gone alone. Though, there was nothing he could do about it now.

"...I thought it looked like something a girl would like," Amane mumbled to no one in particular, scratching his head. He was terrible at stuff like this.

The last time he'd gotten a present for a member of the opposite sex was when he'd given gifts to his mother as a little kid. Amane had never once thought he'd have to pick something out for a girl.

So it doesn't faze her to get a cute stuffed animal from a boy, huh...?

Risking a quick glance at Mahiru, Amane saw her staring directly into the bear's face.

He couldn't tell from her expression whether she was happy, only that her eyes were fixed on the stuffed animal.

"I mean... If you don't like it, you can just toss it," Amane said, hoping to diffuse the situation with some light humor.

Mahiru turned sharply toward him and drew her eyebrows tightly into a frown. "I would never!"

"S-sure, I, uh, didn't think you would or anything."

The response had been so absolute that Amane couldn't help but flinch and barely managed to nod in answer. Mahiru looked back at the bear in her hands again.

"...I would never do such a cruel thing. I'll treasure it." Slender arms embraced the stuffed bear, as if to wrap it up entirely. Amane couldn't decide if Mahiru looked more like a child with a favorite toy or a mother protecting an infant. Either way, she certainly embraced the bear enthusiastically, looking down at the thing as though it were the most precious object in the world.

Mahiru's face was not the stony mask she kept up at school, nor was it the face she often wore when she was exasperated with Amane. This time it was peaceful, soft, and somewhat affectionate—an unmistakably sweet expression.

Amane felt an innocence in her, and her pure smile was beautiful enough to take his breath away. She was really exceptionally cute.

I shouldn't be staring, Amane thought. Mahiru was liable to notice if he kept looking at her like that.

Amane was certain that he wasn't in love, but seeing a beautiful girl make a face like that, and knowing that he was the cause of it, undeniably made his heart throb. She looked so adorable as she sat there with a faint smile, hugging the stuffed animal to her chest. Anyone who saw her would've been captivated by the sight. Amane certainly was, despite his usual reservations.

Just pressing a palm to her face would've made it immediately apparent how much warmer it was than usual. Embarrassed after being so open with her emotions, she swore under her breath. "...Damn." The word was so quiet it could barely be heard.

Fortunately, Mahiru did not seem to have noticed how Amane was looking at her, because her face was half-buried in the stuffed animal that she was clutching to her chest.

She still looked extremely sweet, and Amane was worried he would say something strange in spite of himself.

"...I'm really glad you like it." Thankfully, Amane managed to keep what he said brief.

Quickly, Mahiru turned to face him. "This is the first time I've ever received something like this."

"Huh? With how popular you are, I thought you'd be getting presents like this all the time..."

"What do you take me for...?" It came as a relief to see Mahiru's usual behavior return, but that was only because Amane couldn't see her current expression behind the bear. "...I never told anyone when my birthday was," Mahiru continued, looking back down at the stuffed animal. "I hate that day, so I don't really share it."

Mahiru's expression softened as she looked at her gift, though her words remained sharp. The apparent dissonance set Amane on edge a bit.

"Normally, I hate getting presents from strangers, so I don't accept them," Mahiru explained.

"You're accepting this, though," Amane said.

"...Fujimiya...," Mahiru said quietly, "you're not a stranger."

Face still half-buried in fur, Mahiru looked up toward Amane again. She wore a dreamy, innocent expression. It was captivating, and as Amane gazed at the angel sitting on his couch, he realized he was in trouble.

Mahiru was so cute that Amane found himself reaching unbidden to stroke her hair, and he had to quickly stuff his hand behind his back before he did something really awkward.

...*That was close!* If Amane had let his guard down, he probably would've started patting Mahiru on the head right then and there. Doing something so inappropriate would have destroyed everything he'd built with her.

"...What is it?" Mahiru asked.

"N-nothing," Amane replied shyly.

Perhaps Mahiru had seen his arm move, or maybe she'd noticed his obvious distress as he struggled to keep his alarming feelings from bubbling to the surface. Mahiru's head tilted to one side in puzzlement. That simple movement was enough to leave Amane speechless, and it occurred to him that beautiful girls possessed a terrifying power. Still, he felt embarrassed for being so captivated by Mahiru's cuteness. He was also confident that if he told her how he felt, she would just be confused.

Something about the feeling instilled a sense of danger in Amane, and he did his best to push it deep down.

"…Thank you very much, Fujimiya," Mahiru said in a soft voice, but Amane had already turned away from her.

"Hey, hey, Amane, how'd it go with that girl you got the present for?"

Obviously Chitose was going to pry, since Amane had convinced her to come along shopping with him. The day after Mahiru's birthday, Amane was confronted by Chitose's grinning inquiry.

Chitose was in a different class but had come to his classroom after school. That alone wasn't much of an issue, but hers was the sort of smile that made Amane feel like she was up to something. Today especially, he felt the urge to turn and run.

"Nothing happened—at least, not anything like you're imagining," Amane answered.

It was the truth. He definitely wasn't holding on to any amorous feelings, and he hadn't given Mahiru the present because he hoped it would lead to the start of something more. Sure, she'd graciously accepted the gifts, but there had certainly been no romantic developments of the kind that Chitose anticipated.

"Now hold on," Itsuki interrupted, "The fact that you were so concerned about someone at all is a pretty rare thing, you know. You suddenly have some acquaintance that you seem involved with, and it's a girl. Very suspicious."

"It's nothing like that." Amane knew he had to shut this down now. He was happy that Mahiru had been pleased with her gifts, but he was starting to think that bringing other people into the situation was more trouble than it'd been worth.

Not wanting to feed their curiosity anymore, Amane had answered as bluntly as possible, but Itsuki had his hand to his mouth, as if he was pondering something.

"...Hmm...say, Amane?"

"What is it?"

"Is it possible that the person you gave the present to is...your neighbor?"

Itsuki was smart and very perceptive, which at times like these could be a real pain.

"...What makes you think that?" Amane asked nervously.

"Well, she's the only person I could think of that bothers taking care of you. And you're not from around here, so you don't know many people. Plus, you don't hang out with many girls. She brought you dinner that other day, right? I was thinking that maybe this was about you wanting to return the favor."

"Well..."

"Hmm...Amane has been looking very healthy recently, right, Chi?"

"Oh, I thought so, too."

"She must be bringing him meals pretty frequently, huh? I wonder if that's why he wanted to give her a birthday present, to thank her?"

Amane fought to maintain a blank expression as Itsuki perfectly described the situation to Chitose. It was so accurate that it was like he had been there to watch it all go down. Sometimes Itsuki was scary like that. Amane could see why his friend was so popular. He was a bit of a show-off but also smart and thoughtful. Amane just wished Itsuki would save the grandstanding for his girlfriend.

"What an overactive imagination…," Amane interjected.

"Well, you won't fess up, so imaginations are all we've got. C'mon, spill it!" Itsuki pressed.

"Who knows…?"

"You're holdin' out on us!"

"So stingy!" Chitose chimed in agreement.

"Shut up."

No matter what anyone said, Amane wasn't planning on confirming the truth. If he let anything slip, Itsuki and Chitose would never stop hounding him until he'd spit out the whole story. Really, Itsuki was only the tip of the iceberg; Amane was in the presence of a high school girl who loved gossip, especially when it came to romantic affairs. While there wasn't the slightest bit of romance to be found here, if Chitose got one whiff of the person involved, Amane would never hear the end of it.

Sighing in exasperation, Amane finished packing his things and shouldered his backpack. He'd decided on a strategic retreat, before his two friends gave him heartburn.

"See ya. You two can go ahead and flirt all you like in private," Amane said.

"We were gonna do that whether you said to or not!" Itsuki shouted.

"…Itsuki, weren't we gonna tail him and try to meet the girl in question…?"

"Yeah, uh, you probably shouldn't discuss your operation in front of the target... And anyway, there's nothing to see. Even if there was, you two would never make it past the lobby!" Amane scolded.

"Tch!" Chitose's lips curled into a cute pout, but her eyes were serious. Apparently, she really had been planning on tailing Amane. Nervously hurrying out of the room, Amane left his friends behind.

"...That was a close one," Amane grumbled without thinking.

"What was?" Mahiru asked him curiously.

It was still a little early to make dinner, but Amane and Mahiru had gone shopping and come back to his apartment. They'd been relaxing for a bit, when Mahiru overheard Amane talking to himself.

Mahiru had been acting the same as usual; there was no trace of the girl who'd been so enamored with the stuffed bear. The same placid expression remained, and Amane wondered if perhaps he'd dreamed up the whole birthday incident. Actually, he preferred her this way. He wasn't sure his heart could stand regularly seeing her look at him the way she had the other day.

"Ah, well, Itsuki and Chitose were suspicious about the present."

Amane intended to explain that he'd consulted them about the present, but Mahiru seemed to remember Itsuki's name, and she exhaled, saying "Ah, I see" as if she understood.

"Well, it didn't seem like the sort of thing you would buy on your own."

"That's not what I was concerned about..."

Apparently, no one thought Amane was capable of getting a gift for a girl. If he was being honest, he really didn't think he'd ever experience the many sweet and bitter feelings that were supposed to accompany love all at once.

"My shopping is my business. Why does everyone think that way about me anyway?"

Certainly, Mahiru was cute, and yesterday he'd felt a desire to reach out and touch her. That much he couldn't deny, but what young man wouldn't have felt that way? Mahiru was outrageously beautiful, after all. Amane had been caught up in her beauty; that was all. Nothing about what had happened was evidence he had any deeper feelings. Mahiru was a great person, but Amane was not interested in her like that.

He glanced over at Mahiru. She was just as beautiful as ever, but Amane's heart didn't pound like it had the night before. Once again, he reminded himself that he didn't care for Mahiru in any meaningful way.

Worried that Mahiru would say something if she caught Amane staring at her, he looked down at his phone instead. When he did, he realized he'd received a ton of new texts. Thinking it was probably Itsuki, Amane decided to check them, but it turned out they hadn't come from his friend.

Amane frowned at the sender's name: SHIHOKO.

She was one of only three female contacts in Amane's phone. There was Chitose, Mahiru, and…Amane's mother.

Wondering what she could possibly want, Amane tapped the message thread. He hated dealing with his mother's high-strung questions, always asking him how exams were going or whether he needed anything. He could barely handle Chitose, and yet some members of his family were just like her. In fact, Chitose might become very much like Amane's mother as she got older. Shihoko wasn't so bad that Amane outright hated her, but he couldn't stand his mother's personality.

"I brought some fruit back from Grandfather's, so I'm going to share it with you, Amane. I'm sending it over, so be at your place on Saturday afternoon! I won't forgive you if you refuse delivery or aren't there to get it, okay?"

"So you can just decide my plans all on your own...?" Amane muttered. Now, he didn't actually have any plans for Saturday, but he thought his mother ought to have at least contacted him a little earlier.

"Did something happen?" Mahiru must have heard Amane's whisperings, because she looked over at him with her usual calm expression.

"My mom picked some fruit at my grandpa's place, and she's sending it here on Saturday afternoon. Probably apples and stuff," Amane explained.

"Do you peel your apples?"

"...I guess I could do that, with a peeler."

"That would peel them, but...it'll take off a lot of the flesh, too, so it's a little wasteful."

Mahiru's words sounded like something Amane's mother would say, and he tried to swallow that thought before it surfaced.

"If it comes down to it, we can just eat them whole," he said.

"How savage."

"It's a pain to peel them." Amane shrugged and grinned haplessly.

"You're such a mess." Despite Mahiru sounding annoyed and giving a rather brutal assessment of Amane's table manners, the way she held herself also showed some understanding. "I guess it's all the same once you eat them."

"You know, I'm not sure I'll be able to eat them all before they go bad. Do you want some, too?" asked Amane.

"Sure, I'd be happy to take some. Fruit is expensive, after all." It was kind of a domestic thing to say, but then again, that was the kind of person Mahiru was.

"Saturday, right? In that case, I'll make us lunch beforehand as thanks," Mahiru said.

"But you're always taking care of me already," Amane protested.

"Like I've told you, I really don't mind making food for you, Fujimiya." Mahiru smiled very slightly. Somehow, the little grin made Amane feel awkward. It called to mind the events of the previous day, and Amane couldn't help but avert his eyes from the beautiful angel in his apartment.

"...All right, thanks," he replied curtly.

Chapter 10

Mother Invades

Asking Mahiru to pick up her portion of the fruit as soon as the package arrived turned out to be a big mistake. When Amane heard the sound of the intercom and the high-pitched, mischievous voice that called "Aaa-maaa-neee!" through it, he understood that he was in trouble.

Amane had been very grateful for Mahiru's proposal to make lunch for him on Saturday. It had seemed a veritable blessing from heaven at the time. Truly, the carbonara she'd whipped up had been delicious. The thick-bodied sauce and the kick of black pepper were a perfect match, and it'd been tremendously tasty.

Mahiru hadn't done anything wrong. Those at fault were Amane himself for failing to recognize in advance what his mother had meant by telling him to be home on Saturday for the delivery and that irksome, surprise-loving woman herself.

"…Um, Fujimiya? Is that the delivery…?" Mahiru asked.

"Nope. That would be my mother. She's probably using her duplicate key to get through the front door and is heading up right now," Amane explained. Thinking back on it, it had been his own mistake to take what his mother had said at face value. One way or another, she always created situations that allowed her to come by and check in on him. Amane's mother could never resist employing a little misdirection.

"…Uh, your mother?"

"She probably came to see whether I'm getting along okay…and she didn't tell me she was coming. Probably because she knew I would clean up in advance."

"Uh-huh…"

"I know it's all a bit hard to swallow, but that doesn't matter right now."

Right now, the problem was what to do with Mahiru. If Amane's mother had still been in the lobby downstairs, he could have sent Mahiru home, but that was out of the question now that she was approaching his door. At the same time, his mother was sure to get the wrong idea if he invited her into his apartment and she came across Mahiru. There was no doubting that Mahiru would hate that as much as Amane would.

The longer Amane puzzled over what to do, the closer his mother was getting to just barging right in.

I can't believe this is happening… Amane did have an idea, but he didn't like it.

"…I'm sorry, Shiina, but could you please hide in my bedroom?"

"Huh, wh-what?"

"Take your stuff with you, and once I find some way to get my mom outside, you can go back home. I'm really sorry, but please?"

With no other viable option, Amane took the helm and steered Mahiru into concealing herself. Thankfully, they'd already finished cleaning up after lunch, so that wouldn't be a giveaway. If he hid her shoes in the shoe closet, they wouldn't be discovered, and Mahiru could just bring her personal effects into Amane's room.

The plan was to let Amane's mom to make a quick inspection of the apartment while Mahiru was hiding. Amane would mention to his mother that he really wanted to eat her home cooking, something that'd probably keep her too busy to push her way into his room.

Whatever it took, Amane had to keep his mother from breaching the bedroom.

He would purposely request that his mother cook something that used an ingredient he didn't have in his refrigerator. If the two of them went out shopping together, that would provide Mahiru with a window to escape.

Amane hurriedly explained to Mahiru that such a scheme was the only option as he handed her his extra key and asked her to cooperate with the greatest sincerity he could muster.

"O-okay," she said, nodding in bewilderment.

In truth, the storage room was also an option, but Amane didn't want a girl to wait in there. It had no heating, which meant it was quite cold this time of year. Amane's bedroom had a proper heater, as well as soft cushions. It wouldn't do to have Mahiru sitting on a bare floor while she shivered from the cold.

"…All right, I'm counting on you. I have to deal with my mom, so…"

Even before meeting his mother, Amane looked dejected. He headed for the entrance while Mahiru quietly slipped into the bedroom. After making sure that the angel was hidden, Amane reluctantly opened the front door.

"My goodness Amane, that took you long enough. I'm glad to see you're looking well. I was starting to wonder if you were asleep."

There was Amane's mother, standing just outside his apartment. He hadn't seen her since summer break.

Although she was a parent, it would have been difficult to tell from her looks alone. It wasn't just that her face looked young, she never acted her age, either. She wore the same sort of happy expression she often had back when Amane was still living at home.

"Yeah, yeah, I'm perfectly fine, so how about heading home?"

"How can you say that to your own mother? It took me several hours to get here, you know? Don't I even get a thank-you?"

"Thank you very much for traveling a great distance, now please go home."

"Come now, don't say such things. It's not very endearing. You should act more like Shuuto, your father!"

"Men don't need to be endearing, do we?" While Amane had spat his words acidly, his mother, Shihoko, didn't seem bothered at all, instead breaking into a fit of laughter.

"You've really hit your rebellious phase!" she said. "I hope you're not planning on having me stand outside all day. I'm coming in, okay?"

"Wait, nobody said you could—"

"Have you forgotten that your father and I pay the rent on this place?"

There was nothing Amane could do to argue or refuse his mother once she'd played that card. Reluctantly, he allowed her to enter.

To keep her from going into the bedroom, Amane casually guided his mother to walk past the bedroom door and into the living room.

"By the way, you really should tell me beforehand when you plan on visiting," said Amane.

"Now, I wouldn't be able to get a proper picture of my son's living situation if I didn't show up unannounced, would I?" Shihoko replied.

"Ugh… Look, there's no problem, okay? I'm keeping the place clean."

"You certainly are; I'm surprised. You never kept your room clean at home, but you're doing better than I'd expected. I'm surprised." Shihoko nodded seriously, looking genuinely astonished as she surveyed the living room.

The unspoken truth was that his place was only clean because Mahiru had helped Amane tidy up. Her advice and constant scolding was a big part of how his place had managed to stay clean, too. Really, Mahiru deserved most of the credit, but there was no way Amane was going to tell his mother that now.

"Your skin looks good, too; you must be eating well," Shihoko observed.

"...Yeah," Amane admitted, unable to meet his mother's eyes. Even his improved health was something he owed to the angel.

"You're even cooking properly, huh. Oh, but it looks like you're cooking for two?"

Shihoko's manicured finger was pointing at his dish rack. Two people had eaten lunch, so naturally there were two sets of dishes. Carelessly, Amane had forgotten to put them away. He should've remembered how perceptive his mother could be.

"Yeah, I had a friend over." Amane's answer was not quite a lie. He'd spoken as indifferently as he was able, doing his best to stop himself from shaking. It was fair to say that he and Mahiru had built up to something resembling a friendship, so it wasn't exactly untrue. There was the small matter of hiding that the friend in question was a girl.

"Hmm," Shihoko replied with a tone that suggested she didn't really accept that explanation at face value. She scanned the living room again.

"I suppose you get a passing mark. You're doing so well, I can hardly believe you're a boy living on his own," Amane's mother finally conceded.

Somehow, Amane had been able to deceive her, though only just barely. Strangely, he felt a chill run down his spine, and he was sweating bullets. On the other hand, maybe he shouldn't have been so surprised to have passed his mother's inspection. Mahiru really had turned some things around for him, after all.

"See, there was nothing for you to worry about, Mom."

"I suppose not; though I can hardly believe it. You could barely do anything for yourself at home. You've certainly grown up."

"...I'm basically an adult," Amane replied, though inwardly, he scoffed at himself for having the audacity to say such a thing.

"Good job," Shihoko praised, smiling.

It made Amane a little uncomfortable to hear that, since of course he hadn't done any of it on his own. There was no way he could risk telling his mother the truth, however, so he would have to leave things as they were and try to get her out of there.

She's pretty much finished her evaluation, right? I wonder if I can get her to leave without saying anything about wanting to eat her cooking or whatever, Amane thought.

"That just leaves the bedroom check, I suppose," Shihoko mused nonchalantly.

Amane's eyes went wide at the drop of that bomb. Mahiru was still in there. If his mother found a girl hiding in the bedroom, a far greater disaster would ensue than if Amane had just revealed Mahiru from the get-go.

"Hey, don't joke around. Even if you're my mom, I don't want you digging around in my bedroom."

"Oh? Something in there you're feeling embarrassed about?" Shihoko prodded.

"There's probably one or two embarrassing things in any high school guy's room, if you think about it."

"So you admit it?"

"Yeah, I admit it. Please don't go in there."

Even though it was shameful, there'd been no other choice. Amane had been forced to go along with his mother's assumption to keep her from entering the bedroom. If she discovered Mahiru in Amane's room, she would most assuredly get the wrong idea. For both his own sake and Mahiru's, Amane needed to avoid that at all costs.

When Amane's mother saw him blocking the door to his room, desperately trying to keep her from getting through, she could tell right away that he was hiding something. Closing in on her son, Shihoko said, "I suppose you are grown up, if you're hiding those sorts of things from your parents."

If it came down to it, Amane was prepared to keep his mom out by force if necessary, though he admittedly didn't like that idea. He stood ready to stop her, but then...

Thump. There came a noise from inside the bedroom.

"Amane..."

"Yes."

"What are you hiding?"

"...It has nothing to do with you, Mom."

"So you say." A wide grin spread across Shihoko's face.

It was the kind of coercive smile that could not be denied. Amane became extremely uncomfortable every time she looked at him like this. It had a way of sapping his willpower to oppose her.

Amane groaned, and Shihoko saw an opening. She put her hand on the doorknob to his room, and by the time Amane noticed, it was far too late. Shihoko slipped past Amane, intent on discovering the source of the noise on the other side of the door.

What met her eyes beyond that barrier that Amane had failed to protect was the figure of a beautiful girl. She was leaning her back against the side of the bed while hugging a cushion to her chest. The girl's eyes were closed, and her breaths were a gentle rhythm. Mahiru had dozed off by the time Shihoko discovered her.

A warm room with a heater running and a full stomach after lunch were the perfect conditions for an afternoon nap. Amane couldn't help but wonder whether Mahiru often slept in boys' rooms, but all this really confirmed was that she found Amane to be harmless enough to doze off in his bedroom.

He couldn't exactly blame her for it. Sitting motionless so as not to make any noise had probably gotten real boring real fast.

The main problem was, obviously, Shihoko, who had arrived at just the wrong moment to witness a situation she was sure to misunderstand.

Had he been the third party, Amane would have gotten the wrong idea, too. He would have assumed they were so intimate that Mahiru had no problem drifting off for a nap in his room.

Grimacing all the while, Amane glanced over at his mother and saw that her eyes were sparkling. He could only imagine the commotion she was about to raise.

"Oh my, Amane, you've got such an adorable girlfriend!" Shihoko shrieked in her youthful voice. "This isn't the kind of girl you can just hide away in a corner, you know!"

Amane felt a headache coming on.

She had immediately jumped to possibly the worst conclusion available, and to make matters worse, she was clearly very excited about the idea that her son was dating such a lovely girl. There was no doubt that even Amane's mother was smitten with Mahiru's beauty.

Mahiru looked so vulnerable when she was asleep. The practiced air of elegant refinement that she always wore like a mask had melted away, revealing the full captivating nature of her looks. Her cute face had never looked more peaceful—or more pretty.

Amane had grown somewhat accustomed to Mahiru's appearance, but seeing her like this, he was once again struck by her incredible charm. Her cherubic face held such an innocent serenity. Once again, he felt the urge to reach out and touch her. Her sleeping figure, hugging Amane's cushion tight, awakened many desires in him that were best kept private.

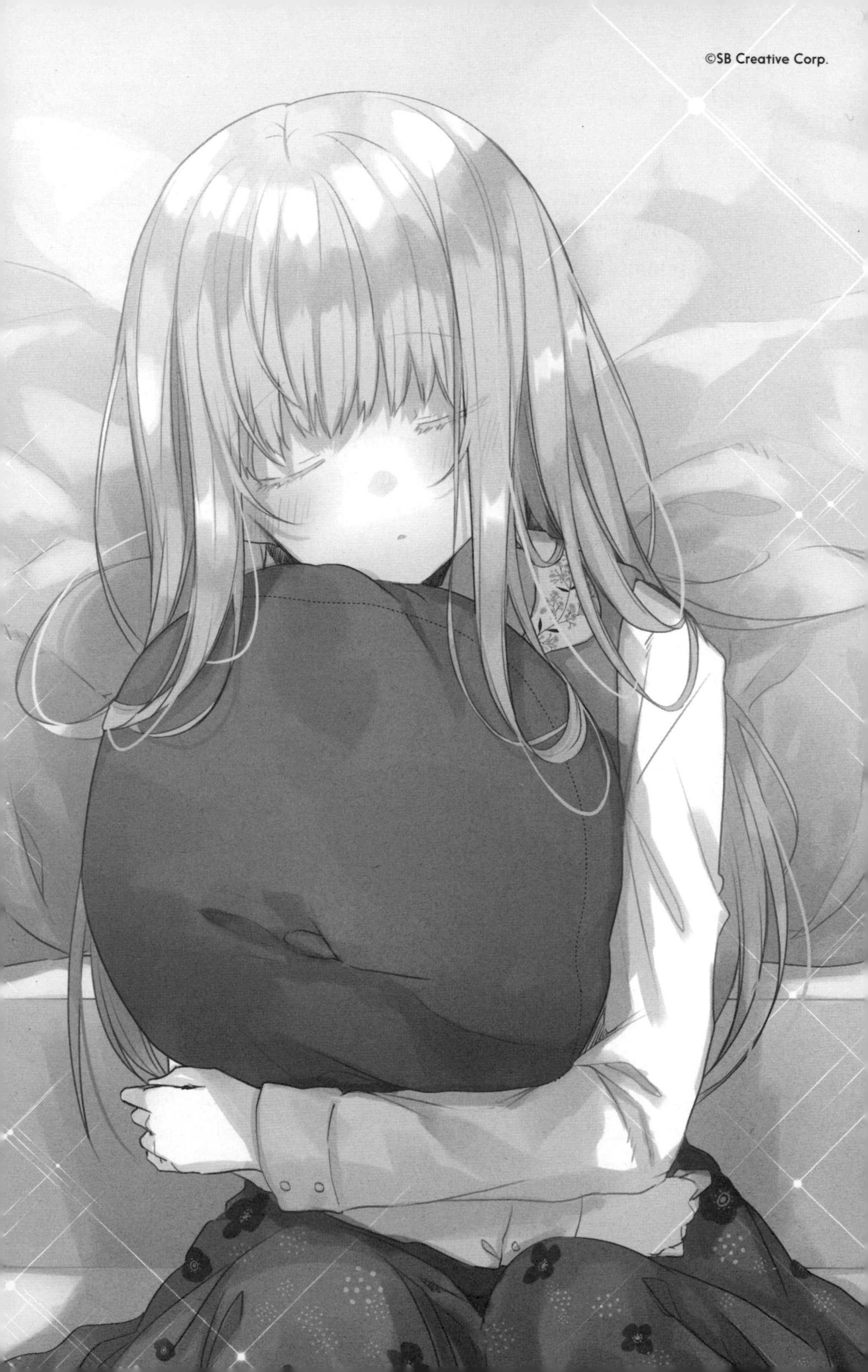

This truly captivating girl was Amane's girlfriend, or so his mother thought. It was no wonder she was excited.

"I suppose the reason you didn't want your mother looking in this room is because your girlfriend is here? Look at you, growing up right before my eyes."

"That's not it! You've got it all wrong! She's not my girlfriend or anything!"

"Come now, you don't have to make excuses! Your mother has no intention of opposing your relationship, Amane."

"No, I'm telling you, that's not the issue here! We're not in a romantic relationship! You've got it totally wrong!"

"Well, whether I'm right or wrong, she's in your bedroom right now, isn't she?"

"That's because you showed up all of the sudden! We were just hanging out in the living room, but I knew you would misunderstand!"

"You see, the problem with that excuse is that you would never let a girl you don't like into your apartment. And I really don't think a girl would just waltz right on into the apartment of someone she didn't like, would she?"

Amane struggled to find a way to argue the issue. His mother was right; Amane was awfully territorial about his living spaces and wasn't inclined to let just anyone into his domain.

The first time Mahiru had come in, she'd practically forced her way, but ever since then, he'd welcomed her over, even when she wasn't coming to cook for him.

I guess that means I really do like her.

As far as Amane was concerned, he was sure he liked Mahiru for her personality, not her appearance. He enjoyed that seemingly contradictory part to her. There was a biting and honest side of her that she didn't show at school, and yet she found it hard to be open about her feelings. He liked her curt and annoyingly helpful attitude and the reserved way she conducted herself. When she was taken by surprise, she would get flustered, and the mask would drop momentarily, which was another thing he enjoyed. Most of all, Amane especially liked that rare angelic smile that he'd only seen cross her face a few times. He supposed that each of those attributes were all precious parts of Mahiru's appeal.

If he had to say whether that was a feeling of romantic love, Amane would have insisted that it was something else, but he couldn't deny that Mahiru was a wonderful girl for many reasons.

"I care about her as a friend. Not every relationship between members of the opposite sex has to be romantic, you know. And I'm pretty sure she doesn't feel that way, either." Amane was not the kind of mama's boy who would obediently play along with whatever Shihoko said. Plus, Mahiru would certainly object to the suggestion that she had feelings for him.

"Now, you don't know that, Amane! Aren't you being rather presumptuous, thinking you know exactly what her heart wants?"

"What can I say to get you to understand that our relationship is not like that, Mom…? Shiina, please, help me out here…"

No matter how he tried to explain, Amane's mother had already made up her mind. Amane pressed a finger to his forehead, stumped on what to do. With all possible urgency, he wished Mahiru would just wake up.

"Nn…"

Either Amane's unspoken prayer had been heard or all the ruckus had, because Mahiru's eyelids fluttered open, and she made a sweet noise as she raised her face. Her flaxen hair slipped over her shoulders. The girl's shining eyes, the color of caramel, were blurry with sleep, and she looked so vulnerable that it felt somehow wrong to look directly at her.

Maybe she wasn't quite fully awake yet as she looked up at Amane vacantly, her eyes still relaxed and drowsy. Amane pointedly stared in another direction.

"Shiina, I don't mind that you fell asleep, but there's been a misunderstanding, so please help me clear things up."

"Misunderstanding…?"

"Hey, hey, Miss Girlfriend, what's your name?"

Mahiru was still clearly confused over what had happened, but Shihoko didn't hesitate to approach her, beaming with an amiable, carefree smile and an overly familiar demeanor.

Mahiru was visibly flustered, still trying to get her bearings.

"Huh, uh, um…"

"It's important to tell each other our names when we first meet, you know!"

"Ah, I-I'm Mahiru Shiina…"

"Oh, Mahiru, what a cute name that is! I am Shihoko; please don't be shy and call me by my first name, okay?"

Mahiru had reflexively given her name when pressed for it. She looked up at Amane, her eyes begging him for rescue. Unfortunately, Amane was helpless. He had been hoping Mahiru would save him somehow. Regretfully, he shook his head. He knew that once his mother got started, there was really no stopping her. She was set on learning more about Mahiru, and nothing would dissuade her now. It was unlikely she'd ever realize just how uncomfortable she was making the poor girl.

"A-all right, um…Mrs., that is, uh, Shihoko…"

"See? That sounds more like my daughter-in-law."

"Fujimiya!"

"That could be referring to either of us, you know? Right, Amane?

"Mom, you're bothering Shiina."

"Amane, you mustn't be so formal with your sweet new girl-friend; call her by her first name!"

Shihoko didn't seem inclined to listen to anything anyone said. Amane scowled at her, but she didn't show any sign of letting up. Her smile was wide and utterly shameless.

"Uh, um, Shihoko?"

"Yes, dear?"

"He and I—"

"Why, I don't know who you mean. He who?"

"…A-Amane and I; we aren't dating."

Even though she was obviously flustered by his mother's verbal assault, Mahiru tried her best to set the record straight. Unfortunately, she'd looked right at Amane and had even been forced to call him by his first name, which was apparently exactly what Shihoko had been after. The older woman's smile grew even wider.

"Well, I suppose it takes time for things like this to blossom. Something to look forward to," Shihoko said, quite presumptuously.

"Eh, ah, um, that's not…," Mahiru said, trying to object.

"Oh no, I must have intruded just when things were getting good!"

"U-um, I want you to let me explain properly! I don't have that kind of relationship with…Amane. We were just having lunch together because Amane can't cook!"

"What a wonderful bride you'll make, sweetie. My Amane set out to live on his own even though he's incapable of doing any kind of housework, you see. So I really do appreciate you supporting him."

"No, uh—"

Mahiru had put up a heroic effort, but she may as well have been banging her head against a wall at this point. The moment she'd mentioned visiting Amane's place, cooking there, and sitting at the same table as him, the sparkle in Shihoko's eyes had changed. The pushy mother somehow looked even more unhinged than usual to Amane.

Once Shihoko got like this, he knew there was nothing he could do to stop her. The only person who ever stood a chance was his father, Shuuto.

"Shiina, just give up. My mother won't listen to anyone when she gets like this."

"You can't be serious…" Mahiru sounded extremely dismayed.

Amane realized that they weren't getting anywhere. Trying to explain the situation wasn't working, and he clearly couldn't stop his mother's wild speculations.

"At any rate, my Amane did quite well to snag such a beauty. I'm surprised."

With Amane exhausted from arguing, and Mahiru having no clear idea what to do, both simply went quiet.

It was possible Amane's mother took their sudden silence as a sign of agreement, though Shihoko had doubtlessly already assumed that their embarrassment was proof enough of her suspicions. She was looking at Mahiru with no attempt to hide the wild curiosity in her eyes.

"What do you think, Mahiru? Can my Amane really make it, living on his own?"

"Uh… That's… Well…," Mahiru stammered. "…Enough to stay alive…"

"You should've just said I'll be fine!" Amane interjected.

"I remember the place being pretty bad," Mahiru reminded him.

"Don't bring that up. I'm keeping it clean now, aren't I?"

"And I've been helping you with the cleaning this whole time, haven't I?"

"That's true, and I'm grateful for it," Amane admitted. "All of it, truly—the food, the cleaning, and everything else." Mahiru was inarguably the reason that he'd been able to live so comfortably, and he would bow down in thanks to her without any hesitation. He knew that she wouldn't have done so much if she'd hated it, but he always strove to make his appreciate known.

As should've been expected by now, Amane's mother interpreted the exchange in a different light.

"Well now, Amane, so it wasn't just today's lunch! Mahiru's been doing everything for you this whole time, you useless child. The way you speak to each other—it's like you're already living together!"

"No! How did you even reach that conclusion?! We only live next to each other!" Amane fired back.

"Aha, so it was fate! Isn't that wonderful, Amane. You got me such a beautiful daughter-in-law."

"I'm not denying that she's beautiful and talented, but I'm totally against calling it fate or destiny or whatever!"

"Doesn't it sound more romantic that way?"

"That's not what I'm bothered by! I'm telling you we don't have a romantic relationship at all!"

"How persistent." Clearly, Shihoko was choosing to believe that Amane was still too embarrassed to admit the truth.

Amane's face contorted into a progressively deeper grimace, and he heaved his heaviest sigh of the last few months. He couldn't recall how many times he'd suffered at the hands of his mother's wild imagination. Shihoko was really the kind of woman who just did whatever she wanted.

As for Mahiru, the one who'd been caught unawares by the full weight of Shihoko's overwhelming enthusiasm, she could do little else than look helplessly back and forth between Amane and his mother, utterly bewildered.

"Mahiru, this is probably a parent's love talking, but my Amane isn't very good with words, and he isn't very up-front about his feelings, but he is faithful and gentlemanly. I'd say he's a pretty good catch. Plus, he doesn't have any experience with girls, so you'll be able to get him to do whatever you want."

"What on earth are you saying, Mom? Seriously, cut it out."

That last bit especially is none of her business, Amane thought angrily.

"I mean, it's true, isn't it? If not, then why haven't you had any other girlfriends? You resemble your father, so I don't think it's your looks. Maybe it's because you're a little immature?"

"It's n-none of your business."

"You really should try harder to act cool in front of Mahiru, you know."

"I will not, and she's not interested, either," Amane protested.

"Oh, come now! Sweetie, you can train him to suit your own preferences, you know. Amane cleans up pretty good if you dress him up."

Shihoko, grinning madly, struck poor Mahiru again, who could do nothing but offer a vague sort of smile in return. Not even an angel could retaliate in a battle like this. Amane's mother was truly something else.

"Mom, you're bothering her. Please go home."

"What a big man you've become, telling your mother to go home."

"I'm serious, please. It's really obvious that you're making her uncomfortable."

"Oh? Is that true, Mahiru?"

"Don't ask her; she'll definitely just say what you want to hear. Just this once, please head back. You can come back some other time."

"Well, if you're going that far, I suppose I get the message. I did barge in while you were alone with your girlfriend, after all. It's only natural you'd be upset to lose your alone time."

"Fine, you can explain it however you like. Just hurry up and go!"

Amane was beyond tired of arguing with his mother, and this whole situation had to be taking a toll on Mahiru as well. He looked over and saw that she also looked exhausted.

Vowing internally to shower her with appreciation later, Amane shooed his mother away and got a look of sour disapproval in return. Even so, Shihoko didn't make an effort to stay, so at least she kind of cared, though it was obvious her view of reality was still quite different.

"Ah, Mahiru, let's exchange contact information, shall we? I want a full report later on how Amane's doing, among other things."

"Uh, o-okay...?"

In a last-ditch effort, Shihoko tried to sink her hooks in again. Caught in the woman's powerful momentum, Mahiru wound up exchanging contact information with her. Now Amane's mother would be able to reach her directly. The thought made Amane want to press a hand to his forehead.

Beaming wide, Shihoko gripped Mahiru's hand and reminded the girl to look after her son. Amane resolved to send his father a message later, asking him to rein Shihoko in.

"I'm exhausted..."

"Sorry; she's like a hurricane."

Shihoko hadn't stayed all that long, but she'd left the two completely ragged.

After flumping down on the couch, Amane put his head in his hands and sighed deeply. Mahiru gingerly took a seat, too, but her usually perfect posture was bent and haggard. Amane had thought that the angel could handle anyone, but even she had no energy left after the encounter with his mother. He was unsure if he should try to apologize.

"I really didn't want to let her go home still believing the wrong thing," Amane admitted.

"Well, there's no real harm done...," Mahiru said.

"No, I think there is... If she was acting like that, it probably means that she's taken a liking to you... One way or another, she's gonna be an issue..."

It was truly unfortunate that this was going to put a burden on Mahiru. Shihoko's love for all things adorable, coupled with her mistaking Mahiru for her son's girlfriend, almost certainly meant that Amane's mother would be finding new ways to poke her nose where it didn't belong in the days to come. Trouble was on the horizon.

"Shihoko really cares about you a lot, doesn't she?"

"That's a nice way to put it, but sometimes she really just refuses to listen..."

More than just an overly affectionate parent, Shihoko doted and fawned on Amane even though he hated it. He knew he shouldn't complain too much, since it was probably at least partly his own fault because he was such hopeless slob. It wasn't as though he was ungrateful for all his mother had provided, but she could be a real pain in the butt, and he wished she'd give him more space.

"...How nice," Mahiru mumbled quietly.

Amane looked up at her. "What is?"

"Your mother is quite a character but also very kind."

"That means she's loud and loves to meddle."

"...Even so, I think it's nice."

Mahiru's words weren't an empty compliment; she really did seem envious as she mumbled and averted her eyes.

A gloomy expression was plain on the girl's face. So much so that Amane thought she might break down into tears at the drop of a hat. Anyone could have sensed how fragile she was right now. It was clearly more than simple exhaustion.

Mahiru must have noticed Amane looking at her, because she suddenly looked up and forced her lips into a small smile. Then, just as quickly, she regained her usual composure and leaned back against the sofa, something she rarely did.

"Mahiru, huh?"

"…What are you saying all of a sudden?"

"Nothing… I was just thinking that it's been a while since anyone called me by my first name. Most people only address me by my family name."

It was pretty surprising to know that someone who seemed as popular as Mahiru didn't actually have any friends close enough to call her by her first name. Everyone at school saw her as a flawless angel. Even Mahiru's acquaintances probably maintained some degree of formality with her, and nobody had the courage to really get to know her. A lot of students only ever addressed her by a nickname that Mahiru herself didn't even like.

"Well, I guess if you don't have any close friends, that would leave only your parents, right?" Amane asked.

"My parents would never talk to me that way. Absolutely not." Mahiru's reply was cold.

Looking her over, Amane saw that Mahiru's face was an expressionless mask. She resembled a beautiful doll, completely devoid of feeling. That, too, only lasted a second, however, and Mahiru's visage changed again when she noticed that Amane was looking at her. Her eyebrows lowered, as if she was troubled by something.

"…Anyway, it doesn't happen often," she muttered, before letting out a sigh.

Amane had been wondering for a while if Mahiru had a bad relationship with her parents. It had been easy enough to imagine that she had problems at home from her frosty demeanor whenever he touched on the subject. Plus, she never went out to eat with her parents and hated her own birthdays, but Amane never would've thought Mahiru's parents were so distant as to not even call the girl by her first name.

Thinking back to how Mahiru had quietly said she enjoyed Shihoko's personality, Amane wondered how the angel must have felt in that moment.

"Mahiru." Rather suddenly, Amane blurted out the word. He'd never called his neighbor by her first name before. The girl in question blinked her caramel eyes. She looked stunned, and Amane could tell that he'd caught her off guard. The momentary surprise had revealed a youthfulness about Mahiru that she normally kept hidden.

"It's your name. Someone ought to call you by it," Amane reasoned.

"...I suppose you're right," Mahiru answered bluntly. A few moments later, a tiny smile appeared. Amane's chest felt fluttery when he spotted it.

"...Amane."

When he heard her small voice pronounce his own first name, the flutter turned to a storm. Maybe it was because, until just a moment ago, his mom was the one calling him by his first name, but when Mahiru called him by his first name face-to-face, he felt the uneasy, impatient stirring in his chest churn and roar.

"Please don't call me that outside, okay?" Mahiru reminded.

"...I already wasn't planning to. That goes for you, too. Don't slip up outside the apartment."

"Understood. It's our secret, right?"

Amane couldn't bring himself to look directly at Mahiru, as she was still grinning a little. Looking away, he responded in agreement and shifted in his seat, turning away to escape the angel's smile.

Though Shihoko's Saturday invasion had been a nightmare, nothing much had changed aside from how Amane and Mahiru referred to each other.

They hadn't suddenly become any closer. Addressing each other a little more directly wasn't a big deal. At most, perhaps Mahiru's demeanor had softened a little, but that was it.

"…Um, Amane?"

Mahiru had come over earlier than usual for dinner on Sunday, perhaps feeling a little uneasy, because she looked troubled.

Amane was glad to let her in, but he was confused by her peculiar attitude. He'd thought that maybe using their first names didn't sit right with her after all, but when the time had come, she'd said his name without hesitation, so there must have been something else bothering her.

For the time being, they sat on the sofa together, and as he waited to see what Mahiru would do, she pulled a handkerchief from her skirt pocket.

As Amane continued to wonder what was up, Mahiru opened the neatly folded handkerchief to reveal a tarnished silver key. It must have been the one he'd given her the day before.

"I'm returning your spare key. In the end, I never got the chance to use it, and then I forgot to give it back. I'm very sorry about that."

"I see."

Apparently, Mahiru hadn't been able to rest until she'd returned the key. Satisfied that he understood the cause for her strange behavior, Amane stared at the bit of metal resting on the handkerchief.

Now that he thought about it, Mahiru came over to fix dinner in his apartment almost every night. Usually, he met her at the door, but sometimes it took him a while. There'd even been times where Mahiru had been forced to wait because he wasn't home. It must have been inconvenient for her to have to wait outside for him, especially during these colder months. Somewhere, Amane had heard that chilly weather was a girl's worst enemy, and now that he thought about it, he wouldn't have been too happy waiting in the cold, either, had the situation been reversed.

Since Mahiru was basically coming over every day, he wondered if it wouldn't be easier for her to have a key to get in.

"That's fine; I think you should keep it," he said.

"Huh?"

"You can give it back to me whenever we stop spending time together."

It seemed perfectly reasonable to Amane. Now that Mahiru had the key, she might as well keep it—but she didn't seem convinced.

"B-but…"

"I mean, going to the door every time you come over is a hassle."

"Ah, so that's what this is about."

"I doubt you're going to misuse it or anything."

"Well, that's true, but…"

Amane had been sharing meals with Mahiru for more than a month now, and he figured that he knew her pretty well. She was sensible, considerate, and kind. He was certain that she would never hand the key over to anyone else or do anything while Amane wasn't around. If there was anyone he could trust, it was Mahiru.

"Besides, you must think it's a pain to have to ring the buzzer and wait out there all the time," Amane said.

"Even if it is, I feel like you're being a bit careless."

"But I'm giving it to you because I trust you."

At that, Mahiru's eyes went wide, and she floundered for words. Confusion, along with something else that Amane didn't really understand, passed over the girl's delicate features.

The truth of it was that Amane had only wanted her to have the key to save himself some trouble, but if she really hated the idea, he was prepared to back down.

As for Mahiru, she looked intently back and forth between Amane and the key for a few moments, then finally let out a gentle sigh.

"…Understood. I'll hold on to it."

"Mm."

"You know, I'm never sure if something is a big deal to you, or if you even care at all, Amane," Mahiru jabbed with a slightly prickly tone. She sounded fed up, and Amane couldn't do anything but smile wryly.

"Suits me well, don't you think?"

"You shouldn't say things like that about yourself," Mahiru admonished.

Amane's smile grew wider. Mahiru seemed to be growing more comfortable with this kind of silly back-and-forth. They were now on a first-name basis, of course. It would've been strange if they hadn't built up some kind of rapport. While Mahiru's eyes were still full of exasperation, as if to say that Amane was really a hopeless case, her gaze wasn't cold. In fact, there was a noticeable bit of warmth to it. She understood that Amane was just joking around.

"All right then, I won't hesitate to use this. I might even do something to your apartment without telling you."

"Like what?"

"…Like…a surprise cleaning!"

"I would be grateful for that."

"…Or how about if your fridge was suddenly packed full of food?"

"It'd make breakfast easier, and we'd have more options for dinner, too."

Mahiru's idea of a prank clearly needed some work. Amane would've been glad to suffer under any one of her suggestions. That she couldn't come up with a real threat even when she truly tried only reminded Amane of Mahiru's gentle nature. It was quite charming and brought a smile to his lips.

"Are you sure you're not making fun of me?" Mahiru looked like she ready to pout, which would've been cute in its own right, but Amane didn't want to upset Mahiru any further.

Suppressing the grin that threatened to break out, Amane said, "Course not."

Chapter 11

A Reward for the Angel

"Well, guess that's how it goes," Amane grumbled as he looked the list of names up and down. The rankings for the previous week's tests were out, so Amane had shown up to check them like the rest of his class.

Coming in at twenty-first, Amane was situated around his usual score. It was a good enough ranking but hardly a result that stood out. He hadn't found this exam any more challenging than previous ones, though it was still a relief to see he'd done as well as he'd expected.

Surprising no one, Mahiru reigned over all the rest from her typical first-place position. She truly was a genius, but Amane knew perfectly well that she didn't attain that position without applying herself. Amane had often seen her studying after dinner. He wasn't about to argue that Mahiru wasn't smart, but he felt confident that it was the hard work that put her at the top more than anything else.

"Shiina is first again, huh?"

"Of course she is. The angel's on a whole different level."

Such proclamations caused Amane to make a sour face.

"…What's with that look? Was your rank that bad?" Itsuki came over, puzzled by his friend's odd expression.

Only the top fifty test scores had been posted. As such, Itsuki hadn't come to see his own score, but rather, to accompany Amane.

"It's nothing. I'm twenty-first."

"Oh? Isn't that better than last time?"

"Only by a little. Gotta consider the margin of error."

"Whoa, you clever people even speak differently compared with us common folk." Itsuki grinned.

"Yeah, yeah." Amane ignored his friend's sarcasm and turned back to the class rankings. He knew Mahiru really gave it her all when it came to studying. She didn't like all that effort to show, however, so she worked tirelessly in secret to make her success look like it came naturally. Others might've praised her or called her a genius, but since they didn't know about all the behind-the-scenes struggling, they couldn't recognize her actual accomplishments.

That must have been an oppressive way for Mahiru to live.

"…I should at least do something," Amane whispered.

"Hmm? What'd you say?"

"Nothing. Come on, let's go back to class."

"'Kay."

"Huh? What's this, Amane?"

Mahiru had gone to the supermarket and returned with dinner ingredients. When she'd started to put them in the refrigerator, a conspicuously unfamiliar white box had caught her eye.

"Hmm? Ah, it's a cake."

It was likely that Mahiru already had an inkling as to the box's contents based on its shape, but she'd gone ahead and asked anyway. Amane had gone to a patisserie that Chitose talked about a lot on social media to buy the cake.

"…Do you like cake?" Mahiru asked.

"Not really. I bought it for you."

"What? Why?"

"I thought it would be nice as a little celebration, because you were top of our year on the test. It's to congratulate you."

Mahiru quickly blinked a few times, unable to process that the cake was for her. She looked quite taken aback.

"B-but I get top rank every time, so it's not really something to celebrate," she protested.

"Well, you're always working hard, so I thought it might be nice to get a reward for once. It's a shortcake. I hope you like that."

"Huh? I mean…I don't hate it or anything…"

"Great. Have some after dinner."

While Mahiru still looked a bit troubled, Amane cut the conversation off there. He'd decided that it would be best to act like this was no big deal, since Mahiru always seemed troubled when people treated her like she was special.

Mahiru was the type of person who would exhaust herself taking care of someone else but then neglect herself. Amane had never once seen the girl do anything enjoyable for her own sake, and whenever anyone praised her or showed appreciation, she'd just redouble her efforts and run herself down.

Simply put, Mahiru was not good at accepting kindness from others. Amane hadn't known her for all that long, but he was sure that much was true. That's why he wanted to return just a little bit of the kindness she was always showing him.

Amane smiled again as Mahiru got everything ready in the kitchen and began cooking for that night.

After dinner, Mahiru put the cake on a plate and brought it over to the coffee table with a nervous expression. Amane couldn't help but chuckle at the sight.

"Wh-why are you laughing?"

"Nothing. Don't worry about it."

"It doesn't seem like nothing."

"It's fine—stop worrying."

Amane found it amusing that Mahiru was acting so stiff, but his laughter clearly bothered her. He was supposed to be showing her some appreciation, not making fun of her, so Amane quickly shut up.

Mahiru set the cake and the coffee she had brought along with it on the low table, then sat down on the sofa.

Her movements were still slightly stilted, and Amane felt another fit of laughter coming on, but Mahiru was sitting next to him now, so he did his best to quash the temptation.

A shy look in her eyes, Mahiru glanced up at Amane.

"Right, so congratulations," he said.

"...Thank you very much. But..."

"It's fine; just enjoy it. You worked hard."

"That's true, but..."

"Come on, eat up. Even you should treat yourself to something nice once in a while."

The deed was done, and the cake was already here. Mahiru couldn't object to that. She gave a small nod before picking up the plate of cake and a fork.

"Very well, then I will gratefully accept this," she said.

"Please go ahead."

With a nimble wave, Mahiru cut the cake into bite-size pieces with her fork and cautiously tried some. Amane imagined that girls were naturally very picky about their sweets, but since he'd gotten the cake from one of Chitose's favorite shops, he was fairly confident it was a good choice.

He knew his hunch was correct when he saw Mahiru's eyes widen slightly when she put the cake in her mouth, then the corners of her mouth relax slightly. Usually, Mahiru's expressions really didn't change all that much, but recently, she'd become a bit more animated, or perhaps it was that Amane had gotten better at reading her emotions.

The mellow, carefree face that Mahiru let show as she slowly savored her cake was one she made only while eating.

"…Hmm? Is something wrong?" She must have noticed Amane staring, and he quickly looked away.

"No, nothing," he answered hastily.

Now it was Mahiru's turn to stare at Amane. Suddenly, she snatched up the fork again, as if an idea had just struck her. She stabbed one bite of cake and held it out toward Amane in a suggestive way. In other words, she was offering to feed him.

"Oh, um…no, thanks, I didn't really want any," Amane protested.

"Really?" Mahiru asked.

"…No, well, um…if it's all right, I guess I'll have some, but, uh…" Amane certainly hadn't expected this development. At a loss, he reflexively agreed.

A beautiful girl, hand-feeding him cake. For many adolescent boys, it would be a dream come true. Unfortunately, Amane's shyness prevented him from enjoying the situation as much as he would've liked.

"You're the one who bought it in the first place, Amane, so you've got to have some, too."

Mahiru seemed entirely unaware of any of the implications behind her gesture. She maintained an ordinary, clueless expression as she held the cake out toward his mouth.

There was no way he could turn her down, so Amane steeled himself and bit down.

An incredibly sugary flavor instantly hit him.

"…This is crazy sweet," he said.

"Well, it is cake."

That wasn't what Amane had really been getting at, but Mahiru remained oblivious.

Sweetness spread through Amane's mouth as he chewed, but he was too preoccupied with something else to appreciate the flavor.

"…This really doesn't seem weird to you, does it?" Amane questioned in a low voice. He was practically gagging on sweetness and shame, and Mahiru was acting like this was all quite normal. Amane snatched the fork from Mahiru's hand and held out a bite of cake to her in the same way she'd done for him.

Turnabout is fair play, right?

"…Um." Mahiru hesitated.

"Eat it," Amane insisted, his tone surprisingly forceful. Mahiru looked even more confused. Perhaps knowing that she'd started this, she decided to play along and timidly took a quick bite. The action reminded Amane of a small bird nipping at something.

Amane stared at Mahiru as she chewed, and gradually, a change came over her. At first, she'd just looked entirely bewildered, but as her mouth moved, a slight redness spread across Mahiru's face. By the time she swallowed the cake, there was no hiding her obvious embarrassment. Mahiru's usually milk-white cheeks now resembled apples, and her eyes were shimmering, slightly blurred with tears.

"So what do you think?" Amane asked.

"I-it's d-delicious…"

"Not that. What do you think about being fed?"

Surely Mahiru understood now how Amane had felt earlier, and her eyes shifted down to look at the floor while she trembled faintly.

"…I feel very much like running away."

"I bet you do. That's exactly the sort of thing that might give people the wrong idea, you know. Save it for your female friends, okay?" Amane turned away sharply to emphasize his point.

"Okay," Mahiru replied with a voice that was barely above a whisper.

She'd probably only fed Amane so easily because she trusted

him. Mahiru hadn't meant any harm by it, of course, but it was still troublesome.

A stubborn sweetness still clung to the inside of Amane's mouth.

Guess someone feeling too safe around you can be its own kind of problem.

In the end, Mahiru curled up into a ball next to Amane, looking slightly embarrassed as she let a small sigh escape.

Chapter 12

Cooking Classes with the Angel

Amane usually bought something to eat for lunch at school, but on days off, that wasn't possible. He and Mahiru each had their own errands to take care of, so it was impossible to eat both lunch and dinner together. Even if it had been doable, Amane would've felt supremely guilty asking Mahiru to make and eat two meals with him.

Usually, Amane only needed to handle his weekend lunches himself, but if he made too frequent use of the convenience store, Mahiru would scold him, saying something like "You need to eat a properly balanced diet." With the costs of his dinners piling up, Amane also felt awkward about going out to eat for lunch.

What to do for his midday meal was quickly becoming an issue.

"...I wonder if I should cook something?"

Without any errands that would take Amane out of the house, he sat at home by himself. Noon was only an hour away.

Mahiru had likely already gotten started making something for herself, but the same could not be said for her hapless neighbor.

When it came down to it, Amane could make something if he really had to. It wasn't like in manga where he'd churn out some censored blob. While it wouldn't look particularly fantastic and might not taste spectacular, the food Amane was capable of creating was edible. It wasn't exactly cooking, but it was close enough, and it kept him fed.

The problem was that he'd grown accustomed to Mahiru's top-rate meals, so the idea of going back to his own dishes was not particularly appealing. Nobody would want to go back to such plain fare after sampling such delicious works of art.

...Augh, Mahiru really spoils me.

Amane had become a slave to Mahiru's cooking. He felt ashamed at the thought of going out to eat again, but he'd also lost interest in convenience-store meals.

Deciding that he'd been depending on Mahiru too much, Amane concluded this was a good time to challenge himself. Even though he'd failed when it came to preparing his own meals thus far.

Mahiru wouldn't be with him forever, after all. Things between them were nice and reliable for now, but there were still two years of high school left, so if anything happened during that time, this relationship of theirs might come to an abrupt end. What's more, they would surely go their separate ways when it came time for college. There was no way things would simply go on like this indefinitely.

I guess I'd better try to put in a little effort now, while I still have her around.

Resolving to do something, even if it was relatively minor, Amane stood up from the sofa and grabbed his wallet.

"Oh, did you go to the supermarket?"

On his way back from the store, Amane ran into Mahiru in the apartment lobby. He wasn't sure if the coincidental meeting was good or bad. Mahiru looked like she'd also just gone out, because she was carrying a shopping bag from the nearby stationery store.

"Yeah," Amane admitted. There was no need to hide it, so Amane waved his supermarket bags to show her.

With a curious expression, Mahiru asked, "Oh, was the shopping from yesterday not enough? Didn't you buy everything on the list?"

"N-no, that's not it... It's just...I thought I might try making lunch on my own," he said.

"...On your own?"

Despite the explanation, Mahiru's eyes seemed full of doubt. It was only natural. Before becoming dependent on Mahiru's cooking, Amane had survived by buying premade meals and convenience-store lunches. It must have been difficult for her to believe that he was really going to cook for himself.

"I don't want to say anything mean," Mahiru continued, "so I'll just tell you it would be safer for you to stop now. What if you burn yourself or get a cut?"

"...You know, it's not like I literally can't cook anything at all."

"Right, it's just that you can't cook anything that tastes good. And that's assuming you don't kill yourself in the process."

Mahiru's thorough dressing down left Amane speechless. She'd said exactly what he himself had been thinking.

"If you say you're going ahead with it, I won't stop you," Mahiru said, "but manage your expectations, or you'll end up severely disappointed."

"...Fair enough," Amane conceded.

By "expectations" she must have been referring to her own cooking. Mahiru was confident in her abilities, and she was well aware how much Amane enjoyed her food.

"It's just that, well, you're always talking about nutrition and stuff. There might be some time in the future when I really have to live on my own, like college. I can't rely on you forever, right?"

Overdependence on Mahiru only spelled trouble for Amane. After realizing how much Mahiru had been spoiling him lately, he felt like he ought to be able to at least manage the basics.

Mahiru's eyes went wide at Amane's words, then she let out a sigh that sounded just the slightest bit impressed.

"...I think it's a great thing to set your eyes on the future, but if you're going to do that, shouldn't you have come to me first?" she posed.

"Huh?"

"Rather than making whatever kind of mess you're about to do without my supervision, it would be much better for me to watch and ensure nothing goes wrong. Amane, are you confident that you won't accidentally destroy your kitchen?"

"...No." Amane sighed. He knew he made a terrible mess of his kitchen whenever he tried to use it. With no rebuttal, he gave Mahiru a slow nod.

"It figures," Mahiru replied stolidly. "That's why it's better for me to be there, right?"

"Would that be asking too much?"

"If I didn't want to do it, I wouldn't have suggested the idea." Her voice had a bit of a cold edge to it, but since she was agreeing to help him, Amane didn't mind. He bowed deeply to express his gratitude.

"You don't need to be so formal," Mahiru said, sounding flustered. Amane smiled, and the two stepped into the elevator, taking it up to their floor.

"...By the way, do you have an apron?" Mahiru inquired.

"No problems on that front. I bought one for cooking class."

"And did you use it?"

"There was really no point. All I did was measure ingredients and wash dishes."

"Figures." Mahiru sighed, as if that was exactly what she had suspected. She accompanied Amane into his apartment. There was actually another apron already there, one that Mahiru had left behind. Amane would've felt fairly uncomfortable using that one, however.

Donning the apron she kept at Amane's place, Mahiru gathered her hair up into a ponytail, like she usually did. Eyes narrowed, she watched Amane put on the dark-colored apron that he had pulled from the back of a dresser drawer.

"Wow, I've never seen you in that before, Amane. It kind of feels like the apron's wearing you."

"Oh, well, excuuuse me."

"I guess there's nothing we can do about that. So you've already decided what you plan to make, right? Since you went and bought the ingredients." Mahiru took a peek at the shopping bag that Amane had set on a shelf.

Amane nodded. "Stir-fried vegetables and an omelet."

"...Veggie stir-fry because I've been scolding you to eat more vegetables and an omelet because you like eggs, right?"

"Bull's-eye."

"It's not like it was a difficult guess. What seasonings do you have for the stir-fry?"

"This: *yakiniku* sauce."

"Oh...straight from the bottle, huh? I suppose it has that robust flavor that boys like...and I guess it is tasty..."

"It's better than me trying to make something from scratch, isn't it?"

If Amane had no *yakiniku* sauce on hand, he'd planned on whipping up something that used salt, pepper, and soy sauce instead. Truthfully, he was glad that he did have the *yakiniku* sauce. Amane whispered a silent expression of gratitude for his good fortune of still having a condiment he could use, then he followed Mahiru's example and washed his hands.

While he did that, Mahiru was arranging all the necessary utensils and lining up the ingredients so they would be easy to use. Truly, the angel's efficiency knew no bounds.

"For the veggie stir-fry, you just need to cut the vegetables up and fry them until they're cooked evenly through, okay? …Do you know how to cut them?" Mahiru asked.

"Are you making fun of me?" Amane replied.

It was obvious he knew that much. He wasn't very good at it, but he could handle a knife.

Under Mahiru's careful supervision, Amane began to finely slice up some cabbage, but he quickly realized how meaningless his earlier words had been after he cut his own finger.

First Amane had been shown how to do it, and then Mahiru left him to try on his own while she watched. He'd done fine in the beginning, while Mahiru was helping him get used to the task, but as soon as she'd left Amane on his own, he'd slipped up.

"…Owww," he mumbled, looking down at his finger. It was only a small cut, but it was bleeding.

The first thing to do was wash it, but of course getting it wet would sting, too.

"…I thought something like this might happen. Here, give me that." Mahiru took a bandage from her apron pocket and skillfully wound it around Amane's hurt finger. He was equal parts grateful and impressed.

"You're very prepared," he complimented.

"Beginners often hurt themselves."

"You have no faith in me, do you?" Despite such an accusation, Amane knew full well that there was no reason for her to think he was even slightly capable. He'd hurt himself almost immediately, after all.

"I do recognize that you were trying your best," Mahiru consoled. "That's wonderful."

"Gee, thanks."

"I still would have liked you to ask me ahead of time, though."

"You say that, but it would've been awful to make you cook lunch for me, too, especially on a weekend."

"I know you're trying to handle things by yourself, but if you mess up and it becomes a whole situation that ends with calling me anyway... It would be easier to have just been here from the start."

"Fine."

This time, Amane had gotten away with only a light injury, but if some terrible kitchen disaster had happened instead, or if he had used some appliance wrong and it stopped working, he knew he wouldn't have been able to deal with it on his own. Mahiru was absolutely right.

"...And please don't ever try to fry anything. You'll start a fire," she added.

"I'm nowhere near advanced enough to make fried food," Amane admitted.

"I don't think it's actually quite that difficult... Once again, I'm forced to wonder how you survived on your own all this time," Mahiru quipped.

"Sorry about all this," Amane replied in a sulky voice. "Now you know why I was living on convenience-store food."

Mahiru looked at him with concern on her face. Amane wasn't particularly disheartened or angry, so she had nothing to worry about, but Mahiru cast her eyes downward, seemingly a little troubled about something anyway.

"...It's just—I'm scared of the idea of you making fried foods, Amane, so if you really want some, please come ask me instead."

"All right then, tomorrow I want to eat fried mince cutlets." Immediately recovering his good humor, Amane was already putting in a request for the next day's dinner. Mahiru gave a small, relieved sigh once she heard that.

"All right, but you're eating plenty of cabbage salad on the side. And I'm making miso soup with lots of vegetables, got it?"

"Yeah, yeah. And…thank you."

"For what?"

"For everything."

Mahiru did so much for Amane every day and still found time to worry about him. Amane was truly grateful, even if he sometimes said stupid, hurtful things. He wasn't sure where he'd be without her. Admitting as much felt a little embarrassing, though.

"You help me a lot," he murmured very quietly. He then promptly turned back to the vegetables.

"Let's eat."

"Sounds good."

Grappling with the vegetables had taken nearly an hour, but it had been worth it. On the table was a stir-fry made from clumsily cut greens, a beautifully shaped omelet…and a pile of scrambled eggs.

Naturally, the beautiful omelet was one Mahiru had made in an attempt to provide Amane with something to use as a reference. While Amane had tried his best to make a second omelet, he'd ended up with scrambled eggs instead.

The failed attempt was set in front of Mahiru so she could evaluate his work. The picture-perfect example, the platonic ideal of omelets, had been prepared for Amane.

After pressing her hands together in thanks for the food, Mahiru grabbed a piece of the tattered eggs with her chopsticks to check the taste.

"…It's flavorless scrambled eggs, all right. Didn't you add any salt or pepper?"

"I forgot. Plus, I was supposed to be making an omelet."

"You scrambled it up too much. What were you thinking, mixing it with the chopsticks until it fell apart? I warned you about that."

"Sorry."

Amane had forgotten to add the seasonings because he'd mixed up his egg while Mahiru was making her omelet. Otherwise, he'd been under careful supervision throughout the whole process. The lacking flavor and shape of his eggs was clearly Amane's own fault.

On the other hand, Mahiru's dish was soft, fluffy, and unspeakably delicious. The difference between them was night and day.

"...I think, for you, it was a really good attempt. The most important thing is that you tried. Still, I'm worried that if I let you try it on your own, the cleanup afterward will be awful, so I'd like you to take it slow, okay?" Mahiru asked.

"...I'm going to become totally reliant on you," Amane replied.

"It's a little late for that."

"Ugh..."

"Just joking. Well, not really, but I like that you appreciate my cooking, and I don't hate teaching you to cook, either, so...really, you don't have to worry."

"...Thanks again—for everything."

It was really thanks to Mahiru's kindness that Amane was able to live as well as he was. He owed her quite a bit, but he knew that Mahiru would hate it if he groveled too much, so he held his head high.

Curiously, Mahiru was wearing a slightly lonesome expression as she said, "If you do learn how to cook, Amane, I guess I'll be relieved of my duties."

It was certainly true that when Amane learned to fix his own meals, there would be no need for Mahiru to do it for him anymore, but Amane shook his head.

"No, that's... I mean... Your cooking is the best, Mahiru, so please... I want to keep eating it for as long as I can. Though, I guess that's kinda shameless of me to ask."

Amane would never have denied it was selfish of him to want

Mahiru to continue cooking for him, but at the same time, her food was obviously leagues better than his, and he couldn't turn it away. The addiction had long since set in, and Amane was terrified of being cut off.

Mahiru's eyes widened at the humble plea, and she smiled slightly. The vague tinge of loneliness vanished in an instant.

"Ha-ha. You really are hopeless, aren't you? Well, I don't intend to stop, so you can relax."

"...Thanks," Amane said, feeling relieved that the shade of anxiety he'd seen on her face was gone, replaced with a faint smile.

"How about I get you to help me out sometimes? Peeling vegetables, measuring ingredients, things like that," Mahiru proposed.

"Like a kid helping in the kitchen."

"Amane, that's where you need to start, you know?"

Since Amane's skill level truly was on par with a child's, there was really nothing he could say back. Mahiru looked amused.

Chapter 13

Christmas with Everyone

"Hey, Amane, can we have a Christmas party at your place?"

"Nope."

The proposal had been immediately shot down, and Chitose puffed out her cheeks to make her disappointment obvious.

Christmas Eve was fast approaching, but since Amane lived separately from his family and was a loner by nature, the holiday didn't hold any real significance. Still, Chitose and Itsuki seemed keen on spending it with him and had come to ask him about holding a little celebration.

Chitose had gone out of her way to barge into Amane and Itsuki's classroom at lunchtime with the idea, and now she had her cheeks puffed out because of Amane's near-instant refusal.

"Come on, Amane," Itsuki angled. "You're alone anyway...ah, unless maybe there's a girlfriend in the picture?"

"No, there isn't."

"Well then, it's fine!" Chitose interjected. "Or could it be that you secretly hate us?"

"Well, if Amane hates us, then I guess we don't need him, either," Itsuki added.

In their own way, his friends were probably expressing their concern for him. There was also the possibility that they were hunting for a place where they could relax and flirt. Amane felt bad about refusing them, even when they made such exaggeratedly disappointed faces at him. He didn't actually hate them.

That was not to say Amane had no concerns, however. First was the thought of how the two of them would act in a private setting. Amane could feel the embarrassment washing over him at the mere thought of Itsuki and Chitose's shameless intimacy. Then there was the fact that he would have to explain things to Mahiru. She would have to steer clear until Amane's friends left, and he would have to be very careful about covering up any evidence of her frequent visits.

"Fine. I get it, I get it. The twenty-fourth, right? I have a condition, though: You have to set me free before nightfall and go somewhere else together to get all your flirting done. I'll remind you that excessive physical contact is prohibited in my apartment." With Amane's concession to the couple's demands, Chitose's face lit up with a smile.

"Guess there's nothing we can do about that rule. I'm sure we can work something out," she said.

"Who do you think you are to say such entitled things?" Amane quickly grabbed one of Chitose's cheeks and pinched.

"Owwsh!" she slurred. "Itsukiii, Amane's buwwyying me!"

"Come on, Amane, don't be mean to Chi! I'm the only one who's allowed to pinch her cheeks," Itsuki said.

"Fine, fine; pinch her real good for me, then," Amane replied.

"Leave it to me."

"Don't you dare!" Chitose cried.

Amane entrusted Itsuki to carry out the sentence, but as one might've expected, he and Chitose turned it into just another excuse to flirt. Within moments, the two of them started messing around, playfully pinching each other's faces.

Now Chitose actually looked happy to be pinched.

Amane shrugged. "…Can I go?"

This was Amane's classroom, but he wanted to get some distance from the lovey-dovey couple before they got any more insufferable.

"No way! We've got to make proper plans. We need to arrange for food and a cake!"

"I'm not making anything."

There was no way Amane could fix a Christmas meal. Mahiru could handle it, no problem, but there was absolutely no way he could get her help this time. That's why Amane quickly brushed off the idea, insisting that it would be impossible for him to cook. Chitose didn't seem convinced, however, and was staring at him strangely.

"What?" Amane asked.

"I was just thinking you look awfully healthy for someone who can't cook," Chitose said.

"So? What's the problem?"

"Well, you see, Chi, Amane's got his own reasons for that," Itsuki commented.

"Huh, well, don't you want to know about them, too, Itsuki?"

"I'll get him to spill later."

"I'm not telling you a thing."

Amane glared at Itsuki as if to tell him not to make promises he couldn't keep, and he laughed out loud, in a forced way. Itsuki knew when to let things go, but he had a bad habit of dredging up old stuff at rather inopportune times.

"You guys are a real handful…," Amane muttered. "Well, for dinner, can't we get takeout or something? We'll have to order the cake if we want one." Attempting to move away from his own affairs that the couple seemed so eager to pry into, he made a pragmatic proposal.

There was no way he could make a cake or prepare a meal on his own, so arranging for ready-made food seemed to be the way to go.

"Ah, all right then, let's have pizza! I'll book a cake from my usual place; they're still taking orders!" Chitose declared.

"You don't want chicken?" asked her boyfriend.

"You like pizza better, too, don't you, Itsuki?"

"True, true. That's my Chi; you know me best."

"Eh-heh-heh..."

While the two lovebirds had decided on what to get without discussing it at all with Amane, he was fine with pizza. Something like that made it feel more like a party anyway. Given the way things were going, they would probably pick up some takeaway pizzas from the shop that Amane and Itsuki often visited.

The moment Amane heard the word *pizza*, he thought of Mahiru—and when she'd nibbled her pizza like a small animal. Amane had found it strangely charming, probably because he usually saw her eating so elegantly. Come to think of it, he'd gotten Mahiru to eat cake the other day, too. Amane's cheeks glowed warmly as he remembered that.

I won't do anything like that again, Amane vowed to himself.

It'd been so embarrassing to feed each other; there was no way Amane could endure a repeat of that. Mahiru and Amane weren't some affectionate couple like Itsuki and Chitose, so the opportunity should never come up again anyway.

"...Hey, Amane, what's up?"

"Oh, no, nothing. All right, we'll leave the cake order up to you."

Amane had drifted back into some embarrassing memories for a moment, and Chitose had started staring at him with a concerned expression, puzzled. Panicking, Amane chased the flustering thoughts from his head and did his best to be casual.

"All right! Let's get our pizza order in, too!" he said, a bit more worked up than usual.

With Chitose's excitable voice still ringing in his ears, Amane returned home and decided to ask Mahiru about her Christmas plans.

"Christmas plans? I don't really have any," Mahiru replied quickly from her place on the sofa. Amane had posed the question after finishing the dishes and joining her in the living room. He'd been confident Mahiru would be going to a girls' party, but apparently, she didn't have anything lined up. Maybe Amane's surprise showed, because Mahiru made an annoyed face at him.

"Basically, all the girls I know and most of my female classmates have boyfriends to go out with. And I always turn down all the boys who invite me out, so my schedule is totally open," she explained.

"Breaking all the hearts, huh?"

Whenever she was out in public, Mahiru kept her guard up, and any hopeful suitors were sure to end up drowning in their own tears when faced with the angel's impregnable defenses.

Still, Amane had to respect anyone who had the guts to ask Mahiru out. No one would be able to do such a thing without a huge amount of self-confidence, and Amane admired those optimistic types.

"...I wonder why boys want to spend Christmas with me so badly anyway?" Mahiru wondered aloud.

"They're probably hoping to get to know you better," Amane explained.

"What for?"

"I mean, because they want to date you?"

"And why would they want to date me?"

"...Probably to do all the sorts of...*things* that dating people do."

"How obscene."

Amane offered a silent prayer for all the guys who'd just been ruthlessly discarded. "Well, I don't think every one of them is like that, so don't be too distrustful. I'm sure you understand that you're the sort of girl who draws all their eyes."

"You're right. It's unlikely that all of them are harboring lewd thoughts. After all, you aren't like that, are you, Amane?"

"Have I ever treated you that way?" Amane had certainly thought Mahiru looked cute, or that he wanted to rub her head, but he'd never gone so far as to fantasize about being intimate with her. If such things ever did cross his mind, Amane was sure that Mahiru would likely notice and pull away from him.

It was only because Mahiru saw Amane as a harmless puppy that he could sit there next to her. Baring so much as a single fang could be enough to send her running away. The needs of Amane's stomach ranked higher in his mind than other appetites, so he had no intention of jeopardizing his relationship with Mahiru.

"I suppose you're right. You never seemed to have any interest in me from the beginning, Amane."

"Mm-hmm."

"That's why I trust you."

"Well, thanks for that."

As a guy, Amane wasn't sure how he felt about Mahiru's reasons for trusting him, but for the time being, he decided he was okay with being the "safe guy."

"…So, Amane, did you have something in mind when you asked me about my Christmas plans?" Mahiru inquired.

"Hmm? Oh, on the afternoon of the twenty-fourth, Itsuki and Chitose are coming over, so I thought I would let you know that, uh, our usual dinner might have to start late."

Having returned to the original topic of conversation, Amane carefully explained the situation while Mahiru nodded along.

"I understand. Please call me once your Christmas party is over, and I'll make dinner then. I'll try to take care of the prep work ahead of time," Mahiru said.

"Sure; sorry about all that."

"It's fine. Have fun."

"...You won't be lonely?"

"I'm used to spending Christmas alone."

Mahiru's casual attitude about spending the holiday alone struck Amane as rather depressing. Perhaps thoughts of Christmas had reminded Mahiru of her parents, because a small, self-deprecating laugh slipped out.

"...Ah, um, this is really presumptuous of me to say, but...even if I can't do Christmas Eve, how about we spend Christmas Day together?" Amane felt extremely awkward making this sort of suggestion. He didn't have any particular ulterior motive, but two people getting together on the holiday usually did carry a certain implication.

There's no special meaning to this, Amane told himself. It was just that he hated when Mahiru looked so lonely; that was all.

Surprised, Mahiru blinked quickly at the suggestion. "Together? Doing what?" she asked.

"Huh? Ah, well, I didn't really have anything in mind. Sorry." Now that it was obvious he didn't have a plan, Amane figured he should drop the issue. There was also the consideration that going out together meant there was a risk of being spotted by someone from school. That would be a huge problem for Amane and Mahiru both.

The best option would be spending time at home, but there was probably nothing in Amane's apartment that would interest Mahiru. It would likely boil down to just sitting next to each other, doing nothing, which would probably be incredibly awkward.

If that's all Amane could offer, he suspected it was probably better to just spend the day apart. As he prepared to withdraw his proposal, he noticed that Mahiru was staring at him quietly.

"...Okay. I'd like to try that," It was unexpected, but Mahiru actually seemed interested.

Her slim finger was pointing at the television. To be more precise, she was pointing at the game console housed inside the TV stand.

Recently, Mahiru had been visiting in the evenings, so Amane hadn't booted up the system much, but it seemed like Mahiru was curious about it.

"I've never used one of those things...," she confessed in a small voice.

Amane didn't have any concrete reason to refuse Mahiru if she wanted to try playing games, but the thought of a guy and girl who weren't dating or anything spending Christmas day together playing video games was somewhat surreal. Even if he wasn't hoping for anything romantic, it was only natural that the idea gave rise to a confusing mix of emotions.

"Oh, well, that'd be fine, but...is that okay? To spend the day gaming?" Amane asked.

"Is there anything wrong with that?" Mahiru replied with her own question.

"I guess not, but..."

"Well, then let's go with that."

"S-sure."

Great, I guess that's what we're doing...

Since it was what Mahiru wanted, Amane resolved himself to do everything he could to make sure it happened. He wanted to at least give her this modest bit of enjoyment. Mahiru was always taking care of him, and she hardly ever asked for anything, so he would let her play anything she wanted, as long as he had it in his collection. It wasn't like he had any plans on Christmas Day anyway, so this was a small price indeed for Mahiru's fantastic cooking.

"All right, we can have a laid-back day that doesn't have anything to do with Christmas or whatever," Amane declared.

"Then it's decided," Mahiru answered.

Amane found it difficult to look directly at Mahiru's smiling face, so instead he nodded and turned away while doing his best to look casual.

"Merry Christmas!"

Christmas Eve arrived before too long.

School had already let out for winter break, and everyone was probably spending the day enjoying themselves. Itsuki and Chitose had shown up at Amane's apartment, party supplies in hand, at around one in the afternoon.

On the table, the pizza and juice they had ordered for delivery were already laid out. The three had actually planned to meet up a bit earlier, but the Christmas crowds had slowed everything down and put them all behind schedule. Thankfully, it was only an hour past noon, and Amane hadn't been waiting too long, so no one seemed all that bothered.

"Yeah, yeah, Merry Christmas," Amane replied.

"Amane, you don't sound very excited! Try again," Chitose instructed.

"Merry Christmas!"

"You're saying the words just fine, but you're not really in the spirit, are you?"

Amane didn't like to be compared to Chitose, who was very excitable by nature.

Realizing that she was even more worked up than usual, Itsuki did his best to placate Chitose. He flashed a flippant, yet still-warm smile at his girlfriend.

"Come on, we don't need to worry about that. Let's get to the eating part and the having-a-good-time part and then the falling-asleep part," said Itsuki.

"You can't sleep here, idiot," Amane snapped.

"I'm just kidding, geez. Besides, if I am gonna sleep, I'm going to Chi's place."

"You'll have to do that when her parents aren't around."

"Huh, Amaneee! What kind of perverted things are you thinking?!" Chi cried. She was grinning, but Amane didn't respond. Instead, he made for the kitchen to grab some cups and utensils. Pouting, Chitose looked briefly disappointed at this lack of reaction but then quickly followed after him, shouting that she would help.

The kitchen was, naturally, neat and tidy, with everything in order. Mahiru had made it her territory as of late, so all the various tools and seasonings were lined up for easy access.

"Whoa, this is way cleaner than I expected," Chitose commented.

"Thanks a lot," Amane responded idly. He took small plates for individual portions and some cups out of a kitchen cupboard. When he tried to hand half to Chitose, he found her staring fixedly at the cupboard.

"…What is it?" Amane asked.

"Nothing!" she answered hurriedly.

Amane felt something devious behind Chitose's sly smile, and a shiver shot down his back. The best course of action for the time being was to ignore her entirely, however, so Amane did his best to act like nothing was wrong. He had a terrible feeling Chitose was brewing up some elaborate misconception, but since she hadn't said anything, Amane wasn't sure what it could be.

Grimacing, Amane and Chitose returned to the living room where Itsuki was waiting. It was becoming abundantly clear that Chitose was in an even better mood than when she'd first arrived.

"Seriously, though, your apartment is super clean. It's so big and luxurious," Chitose muttered. The three friends had mostly finished eating. They'd been listening to Christmas music through the speakers in the living room.

There was little Amane could say in response to Chitose's comment. He was living in a nice apartment because his parents were paying for it, and the place was only this clean because Mahiru had helped him keep it that way. After considering that, all Amane could say was "Yeah, thanks."

"It's definitely impressive how much better the place looks now that it's clean...," Itsuki remarked.

"Shut up...," Amane shot back.

"Yep, yep, I smell a girl!" Chitose added.

"How did you make that jump?" Amane had no idea how Chitose made the connection between his clean apartment and a feminine presence.

"Hmm? Call it a woman's intuition. The way everything's arranged is a little off for you, personality-wise. There's something about the way the books are lined up and how the cords are all gathered to keep them from getting tangled or torn. Plus, there are all sorts of cooking implements in the kitchen that seem like they really don't belong to you, Amane."

"...They're my mom's," Amane lied.

"Hmm?"

Preemptively, Amane had shoved all of Mahiru's things into the back of a cabinet, but Chitose must have caught sight of them when Amane had been getting the plates.

Amane's tableware alone hadn't been enough, so Mahiru had brought a few things over from her place, but Amane hadn't expected Chitose to notice. For better or worse, she was not the kind of person who usually paid attention to such details.

"Well, it's not like we care that much, right, Itsuki?" Amane's reply had been suspiciously slow. Sensing a deeper meaning in that, Chitose leaned over to Itsuki, grinning.

Casually, and without a hint of hesitation, Itsuki reached over and rested his hand between Chitose's knees as he embraced her. It was getting extremely difficult to look directly at the couple.

"Hey, why don't you get a room, you two?!" Amane shouted.

"Oh, you jealous, Amane?" Itsuki asked.

"Psh, yeah right."

Rather than any sort of envy, Amane just wanted them out of his sight. He wished they would stop, but this sort of behavior was business as usual for the couple. Scolding them for it was a waste of energy at this point.

Looking very satisfied with herself as she clung to Itsuki, Chitose leaned against his chest and looked up at Itsuki's face. "…I bet everyone's flirting at their own parties right about now."

"Hey, don't forget you've got a guy right here crying bitter tears of loneliness," said Amane.

There's no way everyone is acting like these two.

There had to be some people who were spending the holiday with family—and others who were spending it with friends. Surely there were even some spending the holiday completely alone. Amane felt like Chitose ought to choose her words more carefully. Not everyone was lucky enough to spend Christmas with other people.

"Do boys really want sweethearts that badly?" Chitose asked.

"I don't think they do," Amane answered flatly. "I certainly don't."

"Yeah, but…," Itsuki interjected, "you're an outlier."

"Shut up."

"Well, everyone gets restless right before Christmas, you know," Chitose continued. "Especially single guys. The other day, I asked the angel about her Christmas plans and found out she'd ruthlessly rejected just about every boy in school. She left 'em all brokenhearted because she supposedly already made plans with someone else."

"Huh," Itsuki said.

Amane had a feeling that someone was him. The idea that he was little more than a diplomatic excuse to turn down other dates wasn't a pleasant one, but he knew that it pained Mahiru to have to refuse anyone. If having plans with Amane helped ease Mahiru's conscience, then he supposed he couldn't object. After all, she wasn't giving his name out, so there shouldn't be any trouble.

"All those poor boys looked so crushed. It was rude, but I laughed," Chitose recalled.

"You shouldn't laugh!" Itsuki scolded playfully.

"I mean, using a holiday as an excuse to try to score a date with a girl you barely know is total crap, isn't it? They're already off to a late start 'cause they haven't built any kind of relationship, so they try to take a convenient little shortcut to get to where they really want to be. Plus, I bet those guys are the kind who'd say they were taking her to a party with a lot of people but then create some excuse to be alone with her. It's a scary thing, for a girl."

Chitose went on to add that the angel was certainly not the type to go along with those kinds of games anyway, then stuck out her tongue and clung to Itsuki even more, as if she'd touched on an unpleasant memory. Trendy and beautiful, Chitose had a different look than Mahiru. It wouldn't have been surprising to learn that she'd had some bad experiences with guys in the past. Amane felt a little sorry for her. Popular girls certainly had it rough.

"It must be hard on Shiina, dealing with all those propositions," Amane said suddenly.

"...You're really not interested in the angel, are you, Amane?" Itsuki asked.

"Not really," Amane replied flatly.

"You already have that angelic next-door neighbor of yours, huh?" Chitose needled.

"Don't think I won't kick you out of my apartment…"

"No, don't! I'm sooo scaaared!" Chitose whined, clinging to Itsuki as she playfully glared at Amane. "So you're not denying that your neighbor has been taking care of you, right?"

Amane's words stuck in his throat, and Chitose grinned with smug satisfaction, though her expression quickly changed when she saw his face.

"Don't glare at me like that! Sorry, geez…" Chitose apologized in a tone that held very little remorse. When Amane narrowed his eyes at her a second time, she gave a cutesy shriek and clung to Itsuki again. Then she happened to look through the window behind her boyfriend.

Something outside was surprising enough for her to stare, so Amane also followed her gaze and looked at the window, wondering what was going on. Little white flecks were wafting down from the blue sky.

"…Ah, Itsuki, look! Snow!" Chitose cried.

"Whoa, a white Christmas!"

Snow wasn't that unusual at the end of December, but it was rare to see any on such a clear day, and it seemed to delight the lovebirds.

It was still daytime, and the temperature was only going to drop as the sun began to set. Christmas Eve was likely to be blanketed in snow this year. Couples all over town were likely rejoicing, and the couple in Amane's apartment had already stepped out onto his balcony for a better view.

"I'm sure you're going to be making out over there for a while, so I'll fix you some warm drinks," Amane shouted as he watched Itsuki and Chitose head outside. As Amane was standing up, a hysterical shriek suddenly caught his ear.

"Huh?! Wh-why are you here?"

"Huh, what?"

"Ah."

The last voice in the bunch was one Amane had only become accustomed to hearing relatively recently. It rang clear and sweet.

Amane felt his stomach sink.

Aware that Itsuki and Chitose were huddling together on his veranda, Amane dashed out in a panic and saw that Mahiru had also come out onto her own balcony to look at the snow. In doing so, she had been spotted by Amane's friends the moment she'd leaned over the railing.

Amane looked at Mahiru, who was now sitting beside him, and sighed.

Faced with the terrible disaster of everyone encountering each other on the balconies, Amane had been left with no other option but to invite Mahiru into his apartment.

No matter what Amane tried now, his two friends would definitely be suspicious. At this point, telling them the whole truth was probably the only way to avoid unnecessary speculations and misunderstandings. Things were bound to get worse if he couldn't keep Itsuki and Chitose quiet about this, too.

"…Um, I really am sorry," Mahiru said gently.

"You didn't do anything wrong."

It was a white Christmas and also the first snow of the year. Of course Mahiru had gone to her veranda to take a look. No one could've blamed her.

If Amane had heard the sound of her opening her glass door, he might have been able to do something, but there'd been music playing in the apartment, so he hadn't noticed. Mahiru had likely been trying to stay quiet anyway.

Chitose was staring at Amane and Mahiru as they reflected on their carelessness, and her eyes sparkled as she leaned in close. "So Amane's next-door neighbor was the angel all along?!"

"Um, please don't call me that..." True to form, Mahiru hated being called an angel to her face and politely objected to the nickname, but Chitose was grinning from ear to ear, and it wasn't clear whether she was listening.

Itsuki, meanwhile, scratched his cheek and looked back and forth between Amane and Mahiru, eyebrows raised. "Wow. So...just to recap, Shiina lives next door, and she's been making you meals this whole time. Is that about right?"

"...Yeah," Amane admitted.

"W-well...um, I had a favor to repay, and I could tell by looking at him that Fujimiya was not eating well, and that bothered me, so..."

The two tried their best to explain how they first met and why they'd continued seeing each other. Itsuki acted like he understood but still wore an expression like he didn't quite comprehend it.

Amane thought that if he were in Itsuki's position, he probably wouldn't be able to grasp the whole story, either. Who would believe that an incredible girl like Mahiru would so casually decide to start caring for an unremarkable slob like Amane?

"Hmm, so I think I understand the situation, but what's really strange about all this is the idea that you don't have any ulterior motives toward Amane, Shiina. Like, you're basically acting as if you're his part-time wife," said Itsuki.

"Guh!" Amane sputtered in surprise.

Wife?

Amane wouldn't have chosen such a word, but he had to admit that their current interactions did somewhat resemble that sort of relationship. Mahiru made him dinner every night and had even treated him to lunch on a recent weekend. On top of that, she sometimes helped him with cleaning. On the surface, it wasn't too far off from stereotypical married life. The important distinction was that neither Amane nor Mahiru harbored any romantic feelings for the other.

Mahiru's eyes had also widened slightly at Itsuki's assessment, but she very quickly recovered from the shock, and Amane could see her slipping into her cordial public persona. "I can assure you that I have no such intentions whatsoever."

Amane realized that she was handling Itsuki and Chitose the same way she handled everyone else at school. Suddenly, he felt extremely embarrassed.

"It's perfectly innocent," Amane added. "Shiina is just helping me out, okay?"

"If you say so, Amane. It's just… What a strange pairing. It's really a bit hard to swallow that such an incredible girl is cooking for you… Hey, that stuffed animal you bought, was that also for her?"

"…Maybe," Amane conceded.

"Whaaa—?!" Chitose broke into a shout.

"Oh, be quiet."

"I haven't said anything yet, though?"

"Your face is loud enough."

"Rude!"

Chitose's smirk was irritating. She looked incredibly pleased with herself for having "solved" this mystery. Up to this point, the conversation had proceeded without much teasing, and Amane was grateful for that. He certainly didn't need any unnecessary prodding right now, and Mahiru likely wouldn't be thrilled by the idea, either. Amane had been hoping that Chitose would keep her mouth shut.

"Come on now; calm down, both of you." Itsuki put a stop to things before they really got out of hand. He'd picked up on the change in Amane's demeanor and was not the type to poke fun at his friend like Chitose would. Itsuki was the kind of guy who was sensitive to how people felt. Of course, Amane wished he'd stopped before prying in the first place, but that ship had sailed.

After scolding Amane and Chitose, Itsuki turned back to Mahiru, who was sitting stiffly on the sidelines, and bowed his head. "...Um, Shiina, thank you for taking care of our Amane."

"Since when did I become your kid?"

"I should be thanking you, for being such dear friends to Fujimiya," Mahiru answered gracefully.

"C'mon, not you, too! You're making me sound like a worthless jerk."

"You kinda are, though," Itsuki remarked.

"Hey, screw you."

He'd heard Itsuki say things like that to him before, but Amane was hardly in the mood right now. Mahiru could have joined in the banter, but she wisely kept silent and smiled, content to watch the exchange between the two boys. She wasn't being quite as expressive as she was when she was alone with Amane, but that smile lifted the veil on her usual act just a little bit. Perhaps noticing, Itsuki looked befuddled.

Amane made a crack about Itsuki checking her out despite his being taken, and Chitose started pouting and laid into Amane even harder. It was kind of funny, but Mahiru had her head tilted in bemusement, so Amane downplayed his enjoyment and assumed a more relaxed pose.

"...All right, look. We don't have a mushy-sweet relationship like you guys do, but I still need you both to understand that this could get really hairy if word got out," said Amane.

"Got it; say nothing to nobody." Evidently picking up on his friend's attempts to point out the potential danger, Itsuki quickly nodded in understanding, much to Amane's surprise.

"You too, Chitose," Amane added.

"I'm not that much of a chatterbox, you know. Besides, no one would believe that such a cute girl is making dinner and stuff for you of all people."

"Well, excuse me for being so undeserving...," Amane muttered.

"Geez, I didn't mean it like that!"

Amane was well aware that what Chitose was saying was true. It was difficult to accept that the star of the school was taking care of an ordinary schlub like him. If anyone did believe the story, they'd probably curse Amane's very name for being so undeserving of Mahiru's angelic attention. Amane was particularly imaginative when it came to visualizing that last part, which was why he really didn't want the truth about their relationship getting out. He could do without all the trouble.

Chitose laughed at Amane's sudden humility. Then her gaze shifted to Mahiru, as if her eye had been drawn to something. Chitose let out a heavy sigh as she stared longingly at the other girl. Mahiru quickly turned uncomfortable, like she wasn't sure what to do.

"Um, what is it?" she asked.

"...It just struck me all over again. Shiina, you're ridiculously cute, aren't you?"

"Huh? Thank you very much...?"

Having praised Mahiru right to her face, Chitose continued to stare, scrutinizing every last bit of her.

"This is my first time seeing you so close-up, but sure enough, you really are as beautiful as an angel, aren't you? Your face has a nice shape, and your skin is lovely and creamy. Plus, your eyelashes are long, your hair is smooth, and you're slim but still curvy!"

"Uh, um...?" Mahiru managed, flustered.

Amane sighed deeply. He couldn't deal with Chitose when she got like this. While the girl definitely had her merits, there sure were some things he couldn't stand about her. He couldn't put up with her high-energy personality or the fact that she was always butting into other people's business.

Amane had a particular appreciation for how difficult she could be because he had someone similar in his family. It was all the ways in which Chitose reminded him of his mother that really drove him crazy. Undeniably, Chitose resembled Amane's mother in taste and disposition; she was obsessed with cute things.

"Wow, seriously, looking closely, you're an incredible beauty—and so cute! Hey, hey, can I touch your hair? I mean, do you have a secret to getting your hair so smooth and shiny? What shampoo and conditioner do you use?" Chitose pressed.

"Wait, ah, um...so sudden...," Mahiru stammered.

"Your skin's so soft, too. What kind of regimen do you follow to keep it like this?"

Chitose, who seemed caught between a desire to share beauty secrets and a want to poke and prod at the beautiful girl, stretched out a hand toward Mahiru as she bombarded her with questions.

Amane felt sorry for Mahiru, who, despite her discomfort, was powerless against the onslaught. Cursing under his breath, Amane lightly bonked Chitose on the head. It was a just a tap, since the goal was simply to get Chitose to cool her heels, but she'd apparently been caught by surprise as she cried "Oww!" and drew her hand back away from Mahiru. As for Mahiru, she seemed relieved by Amane's intercession. He'd forgotten about it because she was conducting herself with her usual angelic poise, but Mahiru was extremely wary around people she wasn't used to. Chitose was a girl, so Mahiru wasn't as wary as she had been with Amane, but her fear of strangers was still quite clear.

"I can't believe you did that!" Chitose whined.

"She's shy, and you've only just met her, so stop trying to touch her," Amane chided.

"I can touch her once we get to know each other?"

"You'll need to ask Shiina about that. Be respectful."

Mahiru had obviously been getting ready to make a run for it. It was a good thing he'd stepped in. Even Chitose seemed to understand why she should stop when she saw how clearly shaken Mahiru was.

"I'm sorry; I got too excited and almost did something without asking," Chitose apologized.

"Ah, mm-hmm..." Mahiru still seemed upset by the close call, and she looked at Amane as if she didn't know what to do, her eyes pleading for help.

"Uh, Shiina, Chitose can be sorta a handful, but she's not a bad person...I think," Amane explained.

"Is that supposed to be a compliment?" the excitable girl snapped.

"Look at the way you were acting. Can you really argue?"

"Nope!"

Chitose, having just openly disavowed her own actions, stared at Mahiru for a moment, then once again extended a hand toward her, wearing a very serious expression.

"In that case, it's a pleasure to make your acquaintance!" This time, however, she presented Mahiru with an open hand.

"Huh? Y-yeah, nice to meet you..." Mahiru hesitantly accepted the handshake.

Once Chitose took a liking to someone, Amane knew she was determined to be their friend, whether they wanted it or not. Something told Amane that Mahiru would be swayed by Chitose's persistence. Really, as long as she didn't do anything too weird in her pursuit of Mahiru's friendship, Amane didn't mind. An ordinary, low-key relationship was best.

"First impressions are so important for becoming good friends, you know! You probably already know who I am, and I'm sure you've heard my name from Amane, but I'm Chitose Shirakawa. I'm Itsuki's girlfriend. I guess you could call him...Amane's best friend?"

"Oh my, I'm blushing! A best friend, wow," Itsuki ribbed.

"Don't act so flattered, Itsuki; it's weird," Amane shot back.

"There you go again... Hey, Amane, they've got a name for people like you, y'know...sweet and sour!"

"I'll seriously kick you out."

"Forcing us outside in the snow? Oh, how cruel!"

"Don't try to wheedle your way out of this one."

Itsuki cackled with laughter, and Amane looked even more annoyed. Mahiru's eyes went wide as she watched their exchange.

"Oh, we always act like this," Itsuki informed her as he smiled cheerfully. "So anyway, I'm Itsuki Akazawa. I'm best friends with that knucklehead over there. If Amane ever does anything stupid or weird, you can come talk to me any time."

"Is that any way to talk about your best friend?" Amane said.

"...Well, Fujimiya doesn't seem to have any interest in me," Mahiru said. "He may not have any basic life skills, but he's an otherwise ordinary guy, so I'm not expecting any trouble."

"Thanks, I guess...but you could have left out the part about me being incompetent." Amane could have gone without that specific remark, but he was happy to hear that Mahiru did indeed see him as a person she could trust.

Itsuki drew close and whispered in Amane's ear, "You've gotten awfully close to Shiina for somebody who says he's not interested."

Amane would be lying if he said he wasn't interested at all, but he really wasn't actively trying to steer their relationship in that direction. He was certain that Mahiru just wanted a close friend, not a romantic partner. The two of them were happy spending their time together as they had been.

Glancing at Mahiru, Amane saw that she'd gotten all flustered again. Chitose had begun another round of interrogation, having decided her conversation with Amane was over.

However, Mahiru didn't seem to hate the attention, and Amane hoped that maybe when she got more comfortable, she might relax a little.

As bewildered as she was, Mahiru responded to the barrage of questions with a small smile. It came as no small relief for Amane that the two girls were getting acquainted without any issue.

"I'm really sorry."

After night had fallen, and Itsuki and Chitose had gone home, Amane apologized to Mahiru, who looked more than a little worn-out.

It was obvious that Mahiru had been left exhausted and confused after dealing with two strangers who'd just discovered their secret. This conversation felt like an exact repeat of the one they'd had after Shihoko's surprise visit.

"No, my own carelessness was what caused it, after all," Mahiru refuted.

"They sure did make a fuss."

"They're...lively people."

"You can be honest; they're both loudmouths."

"They were a little assertive, but they're interesting."

"'A little' is being very generous... Well, as long as you didn't mind, I guess it's all good."

Amane was convinced that his friends' behavior had crossed the line for Mahiru, but the mild-mannered girl was taking it all in stride. He was glad that she hadn't found them too troublesome, but he wasn't sure whether it was a good thing that she and Chitose were apparently becoming friends.

Chitose is a totally different type of girl from Mahiru. Very...energetic? Which is nice, I suppose. He trusted Chitose not to do anything malicious, but he would need to keep an eye on her to be certain she gave Mahiru enough space.

"I don't have any people like that in my life, so it was kind of fun."

"Right, I imagine you don't really have anyone like Chitose in your circle… If she gets too persistent, you can just slap her, okay?"

"I w-would never resort to violence, so I'll do my best to keep her in check with my words."

Chitose had an excess of energy and often let her enthusiasm get the better of her. Amane was sure that eventually his advice would be warranted. As he fixed in his mind an oath to caution Chitose directly the next time he saw her, Amane turned toward the window and watched the snow fluttering down.

If it weren't for this weather, we never would've been discovered, he thought. Snowflakes were supposed to carry good tidings for lovers everywhere, however, so Amane didn't think it right to curse them for his troubles.

Mahiru also seemed to enjoy watching the snow because, once she realized what Amane was looking at, she stared out the window in the exact same way.

It was winter, so the sun had set early. The sky was dark, and the snow was pale, and he could just barely see the flakes falling in the light coming from the surrounding apartment buildings.

"A white Christmas, huh?" Mahiru said.

"Yeah, I guess so," Amane answered. "Though, that sappy stuff doesn't have much to do with us."

"It's still very pretty. Isn't that enough?"

Spending a romantic white Christmas together didn't mean anything to them, since they weren't a couple, but…Mahiru seemed to be enjoying the sight anyway, so the snow couldn't be all bad.

The dancing snowflakes lightly dusted the surroundings, leaving the dark world coated in a powdery whiteness. At the rate it was falling, the chance of the snow really piling up didn't seem very high.

"If it's too heavy, though, public transit will shut down, so I hope it's only a light snow," Mahiru commented.

"That's very pragmatic of you," Amane remarked.

"People can't survive on romance alone," Mahiru answered.

"You're exactly right."

Albeit in an unusual way, the snow had brought them closer together, after all.

They both smiled slightly, and Mahiru stood up.

"All right then, I'll bring dinner over."

"Huh, bring it over?"

"I made beef stew at my place earlier. I thought for sure that if I roasted a whole turkey, the two of us wouldn't be able to finish it…"

"It would never have even occurred to me to roast a turkey."

"You're just bad at cooking, Amane. For lunch tomorrow, I was thinking we could make omelet rices with beef stew on top."

"That sounds so delicious…" Amane's mind had already leaped straight past tonight's dinner and had started looking forward to tomorrow's lunch. "I like my eggs cooked hard."

"What a coincidence; I've always preferred them that way, too. Okay, I'm bringing the stew pot over."

Mahiru sauntered out of Amane's apartment and headed back to her own place for a moment. Vacantly, Amane watched her as she left, reflecting on the turbulent day.

He really hadn't expected to be discovered. His friends might have suspected that something was up, and Amane had anticipated them growing curious, but he never would've expected that Mahiru would simply step right onto center stage.

Part of him wished that their relationship could've stayed their secret for just a little while longer.

What am I thinking? Amane wondered. It was better this way. He no longer had to hide everything from Itsuki and Chitose, which made his life much easier. So then why did he feel a bit wistful? Where was this strange feeling coming from? Though everything had turned out okay, some part of Amane was still agitated, and he needed to relax.

"Did something happen?" Mahiru had returned, holding the stew pot, and she tilted her head questioningly as she stared at Amane with a confused look.

"...It's nothing." Amane straightened out his expression, but Mahiru still seemed puzzled for a good while by the expression she had spotted on his face.

"...Phew, that was good."

Unsurprisingly, Mahiru's cooking had been delicious. With it being Christmas, she had made even more elaborate dishes than usual. She had turned the rest of her carefully simmered beef stew into a pot pie, which she and Amane had shared.

Splitting the pie open and eating the crispy, textured crust together with the rich sauce of the beef stew could only be described as a moment of sublime bliss.

Mahiru had apparently prepared the pie dough especially for this. Truly impressed by her culinary prowess, Amane loosed a contented sigh while polishing off his second pastry of the day, another product of Mahiru's skilled hands.

While making the dough for the pot pie, Mahiru had apparently taken the opportunity to prepare another type of sweet dough at the same time. She'd used it to make handmade mille-feuille for dessert. This girl was already working at a professional level.

"I'm glad you like it... You sure ate plenty," Mahiru observed.

"Mm. Because it was delicious," Amane replied.

"Thank you for saying so."

Amane had grown accustomed to seeing the faint, relieved smile that emerged on Mahiru's face whenever he complimented her food. He had made it his daily mission to see that expression, as it was so much softer than her usual reserved countenance. Though an embarrassing thought, Amane liked to think of it as a special kind of smile reserved just for him.

"...So tomorrow we're having omelets over rice, huh...? I'm really looking forward to it."

"You really do like eggs, don't you? You tore into those rolled dashi omelets with incredible enthusiasm."

"They were delicious; I couldn't help it."

Even though eggs were one of his favorite foods, Amane couldn't stand them if they were badly cooked. The fact that he'd wolfed them down was just more proof of Mahiru's excellent preparation.

Though Amane recognized that it was awfully selfish to be keeping her cooking all to himself, he was not inclined to share with anybody else. The plan was to keep enjoying it for as long as possible.

"...Amane, you look super happy when you're eating, you know?" Mahiru said.

"Of course, because your cooking is so good," he replied.

"I'm flattered, but...really, it's nothing that special."

"No, it definitely is... You need to get a better sense of your own worth..."

This was the homemade food of an angel; there were more than a few boys who'd do anything to have some.

"But to me, this is just the stuff I make every day."

"I'm a lucky guy."

"...Why's that?"

"Because the stuff you make every day is so delicious."

Amane was a boy ruled by his stomach, and being able to enjoy delicious, freshly made meals so regularly was, for him, the ultimate happiness.

"How did you get so good at cooking anyway?" Amane asked.

"Someone important to me once said 'Make sure you grab any-one who makes you happy by the stomach,' and I took those words to heart," Mahiru answered.

"Sorry you ended up grabbing me instead."

"I'm thinking of it as a rehearsal." Mahiru's candor caught Amane by surprise. A small smile spread across her lips.

"...But seriously, whoever taught you must have been amazing."

"That's right; they were an incredible cook. I'm still no match for them. Their cooking tasted like pure happiness." Mahiru took on a faraway look with a gentle smile. The expression felt reassuring to Amane.

From the way Mahiru described it, the person in question had obviously loved her very much, and Amane could tell that Mahiru had idolized them as well. She must have been really lucky to have someone like that in her life.

"I bet it was really good," Amane said, nodding. "But you know... to me, your cooking is what tastes like happiness."

Leaving his mother aside for the moment, Amane's father was a decent cook, but Mahiru's dishes suited Amane's tastes better. Mahiru's cooking was comforting yet exciting, with a relaxing flavor that he didn't think he could get tired of, even if he had it three times a day for the rest of his life. No matter how much he ate, he just wanted more and more.

Though, of course, he could never say that. It'd put too much of a burden on Mahiru.

Suddenly, the girl stiffened. She looked like she'd been attacked in an unguarded moment. She stared at Amane with an innocent and somewhat vacant expression.

"...Mahiru?" Amane asked.

"Ah...it's nothing." Snapping back to her senses, Mahiru quickly shook her head, then stared down at the floor. Hugging her favorite cushion tight, she let out a soft sigh. Something about her had completely changed in the last few seconds. It was strangely endearing.

"What's up?" Amane asked.

"...It's just—to think that someone like me could make something taste like happiness..."

"I don't know why you're putting yourself down, but your food is so good that I want to eat it every day."

"Th-thank you." Mahiru looked up at Amane with a bit of a bashful look and a small grin. The sight of it filled Amane with the urge to hide his face.

This kind of expression was rare for Mahiru, but it inevitably set Amane's heart rattling in his chest, even though he'd constantly told himself that he wasn't interested in her like that. Seeing Mahiru's smiling visage stripped of its usual stony mask made him suddenly feel hot, and Amane worried that she would notice and get embarrassed herself.

"Say, um, Mahiru?"

"Yes?"

"Tomorrow we'll be meeting up around lunchtime, right?"

Unable to stand the atmosphere any longer, Amane forced a change of subject. Mahiru didn't seem to take much notice, however, and she idly considered what Amane had asked.

"Yes, that's the plan, isn't it? We'll make lunch, then play games like we promised... That was it, right?"

"Yeah."

"Unless...you don't want to?"

"No, I was just confirming. Really, even though we spent Christmas Eve together, are you sure it's okay to spend your next day with me, too?"

"If I hated the idea, I wouldn't have suggested it... I'm looking forward to it." Another small smile appeared on the gentle curve of Mahiru's lips.

"Y-yeah," Amane muttered. It was all he could do to turn away and hide his growing embarrassment.

Chapter 14

Christmas for Two

When Mahiru arrived at Amane's apartment the following day, she seemed a little restless. It would've been perfectly understandable to be nervous about visiting the home of a member of the opposite sex on a holiday, but that didn't seem to be it.

Mahiru wants to play games. She's probably just excited.

Apparently, this would be her first time ever playing a video game. In some ways, she was like a sheltered highborn young lady who knew little of the world at large.

"Before we play, I'll make lunch, okay?" Mahiru confirmed.

"Mm. I'll have mine well-done, please," Amane answered casually.

"I know; I remember."

Even dealing with such a demanding customer didn't seem to dampen the girl's mood. With a flutter of her apron, she headed for the kitchen and began preparations for lunch. From the way she was behaving, Mahiru seemed to be quite pleased.

Amane felt a little awkward and embarrassed about how much he had been looking forward to this.

It's just because I'm looking forward to enjoying the games, that's all, he told himself. It certainly was not that he had been excited about spending time alone with the next-door angel. As he watched Mahiru's ponytail swaying back and forth, Amane smiled wryly to himself.

"...How are you supposed to hold it?"

After lunch, the two of them settled on the sofa in front of the TV. Both were now looking straight at the screen.

When Amane had asked her what game she wanted to play, it became apparent that Mahiru didn't even know where to start, so he'd booted up a well-known 2D game and handed her a controller. Unfortunately, Mahiru immediately got flustered as it became apparent that she had no idea what to do with it.

"Uh, okay, so you move around with this joystick, and you jump with this button..."

Mahiru, usually so calm and collected, was looking back and forth between the controller and the TV as she manipulated her character on-screen. It was obvious that this was her first time. She charged straight at the enemies without dodging, dying over and over again. Amane began to wonder if perhaps there were things even an angel couldn't do, though she did seem to be gradually improving, if ever so slowly.

"...I can't win," Mahiru professed.

"Never mind clearing the stage—you haven't even defeated the first enemy," Amane observed.

"Oh, shut up."

"Well, it's just a matter of practice; you gotta keep trying. Get that muscle memory."

Amane warned Mahiru that it would be a challenge, but she didn't seem ready to give up. It was charming to watch the girl tackle the game with such a serious expression. Amane couldn't help but smile.

Unfortunately, Mahiru was just too much of a beginner and kept on losing. Eventually, it was obvious that she was growing frustrated. As she shot a glance at Amane, he could have sworn he heard a game-like sound effect accompany her sullen face.

"Ah, here, you need to do it like this…" Mahiru was sure to lose interest if she continued to metaphorically bash her head against a wall, so Amane put his hand on the controller she was holding and tried to physically show her what to do.

Amane had cleared this game on countless occasions, so he was able to help Mahiru get through tough spots. Surprisingly, Mahiru was actually worse than the average player. Most people wouldn't have gotten stuck nearly as many times as she did, but Amane kept that thought private.

"Look, this enemy moves at a consistent speed in an irregular pattern, but if you watch here, he moves toward your character and speeds up as he approaches. Just watch your timing and jump."

Amane put his hand over Mahiru's smaller one and gripped the controller to manipulate the character on the TV, showing her how as he explained. On the screen, the game character moved as Amane had said it would, avoiding the oncoming enemy.

It wasn't much of a move, but it was apparently enough to impress Mahiru, who let out a small gasp of astonishment. Her eyes, rimmed with long lashes, snapped wide open, and her expression brightened.

The two were sitting closer together than they ever had before, and Amane noticed for the first time that Mahiru's lower lashes were fairly long, too. Smiling, he watched Mahiru happily play.

As Amane admired her beautiful profile, Mahiru turned toward him, possibly because she'd felt his eyes on her. He'd needed to get close in order to be able to reach the controller, so the two had ended up far nearer to each other than either had expected. Their arms and hands were even touching, and Amane could feel Mahiru's breath lightly grazing his skin. Amane found himself surrounded by warmth and a faint, sweet fragrance.

"S-sorry..." Amane suddenly realized that his hands were almost completely covering Mahiru's, and he pulled away in a panic, while Mahiru's eyes darted around the room as if she had only just realized they were touching at all.

Blinking dramatically, Mahiru replied, "No...it's fine. I'm the one who should apologize."

The girl's cheeks had flushed scarlet, and Amane was filled with regret over what he'd done.

Mahiru wasn't a fan of physical contact. No matter how used to each other they had gotten, having someone touch her hands like that had probably been too much for her. Thankfully, while she looked fairly embarrassed, she didn't appear upset or angry.

"Really, I'm sorry," Amane said again.

"Um, I'm not that bothered by it...," Mahiru said.

"Don't you hate physical contact?"

"...I was surprised but not upset. It's not like you're a stranger."

It seemed that today, the magnanimous angel had seen fit to forgive Amane's transgression. Relieved at how easily Mahiru let it go, Amane restarted the game.

Fixing his eyes on the TV screen, Amane got ready to help Mahiru make some real progress in the game this time. Then he saw that her character had fallen off the stage—a rather predictable outcome. Amane was seriously beginning to wonder if he could do anything to help her get better.

In the end, Mahiru somehow managed to clear one level, whining all the while. The two of them agreed that was probably a good stopping place for the time being.

If Amane kept making a total beginner face death, it would have a considerable effect on her motivation. His plan for now was to get her to try another game and loosen up.

"Mahiru, you're tilting."

To that end, next Amane had suggested a racing game, since that had some grounding in the real world, but Mahiru was leaning with her entire body.

There was no gyroscopic control element to the game, so there was absolutely no need to physically move around. Amane wasn't sure whether Mahiru even noticed what she was doing, but she swayed left and right with every turn she made in the game.

In contrast to the earlier game, this one was all about driving a car, and Amane had thought it'd be easier, since pretty much everyone understood the concept of driving to some degree. Playing through the tutorial also might've helped, because even though Mahiru's driving was a bit clumsy, she was able to handle the actual gameplay.

She was trying her absolute hardest to perform well. Her body swayed this way and that while she maintained a very serious expression.

This is ridiculously cute, Amane thought.

Mahiru was strangely adorable, rocking back and forth like a pendulum. Her intense focus and effort only made her look even cuter.

With every turn, Mahiru's body automatically leaned way to the side. Eventually, she tumbled right onto Amane's lap, and he was forced to choke down a laugh.

"...You really don't need to tilt your whole body, you know?" he said.

"I-it wasn't on purpose," Mahiru replied sheepishly.

"Yeah, I know. But still, you were leaning pretty far."

Mahiru sat back up, somehow keeping her trembling, pouty lips in check.

The girl had felt soft and light when she'd accidentally flopped on him. That much was to be expected as Mahiru had a small build, but she was so slim that sometimes Amane worried she might snap in half.

Roused out of Amane's lap, Mahiru's cheeks were flushing, and her body was trembling, likely from embarrassment. It was times like these that the girl really resembled a small animal.

Finally, Amane couldn't stand it anymore, and he burst into a fit of laughter.

"A-are you making fun of me?" Mahiru demanded.

"No, no. I was just thinking how charming you are."

"So you *are* making fun of me!"

"You think I'd mock someone while they're trying their best?"

"No, but..."

"See? You were just very cute; that's all."

"...When you say cute, I'm sure you mean childish."

There was a bit of a peevish overtone to Mahiru's words, and Amane was worried she might get depressed if he teased too much; thus he decided to keep any further thoughts to himself. He flashed Mahiru a half smile in response to her expression of disapproval, and she quickly turned away.

Any trace of the angel's gloomy mood vanished instantly when she returned to the game. Her intense concentration overrode everything else on her face. It was becoming clear that she was getting used to the game, as she was managing to keep up with the other cars, if a little awkwardly. Amane had been right to assume a more familiar concept like steering a car was better for Mahiru. She did still veer off course into the dirt or slam into a wall a few times, though.

Amane had been worried she might end up running the whole course backward, since she'd never played a game before, but he was relieved to see that she was making better progress than he'd expected.

Trying to play the racing game together with Mahiru proved to be a little difficult, as she kept distracting Amane without realizing it. As she tilted her whole body back and forth with the game, she occasionally leaned right into him. Each time she did so, a lovely scent would waft over him, making it difficult to keep his composure.

Even with the unusual handicap, Amane still managed to maintain a huge lead. They were competing against the weakest computer opponents, after all.

"...How are you so fast?" Mahiru inquired.

"Practice and experience," Amane replied.

After playing the game so many times, Amane knew the course by heart and understood how to best navigate the turns. Even with Mahiru's outside interference, he was able to seize every advantage and hold the lead without much trouble.

Glancing back at Mahiru, who appeared utterly dumbstruck, Amane quietly switched the game to solo mode and dropped out of the competition. Mahiru didn't have enough experience, so Amane thought it'd be better to play together after he let her practice by herself for a while. It was better that she got comfortable playing against computer-controlled characters rather than feel disappointed over losing to Amane.

Thankfully, it was clear that Mahiru had no shortage of determination, and she stared enthusiastically at the screen even after going to solo play. With an attitude like that, Amane was sure she would quickly learn to hold her own against a computer opponent.

It was obvious what a hard worker she was, even with something like a video game. Such perseverance was rather charming, but whenever Amane let a smile slip onto his face, Mahiru would quickly take notice and slap his knees in protest.

If he laughed too much, amused by her protests, Mahiru would frown and grumble, "Amane, you idiot."

*　　*　　*

"I won."

After two hours of dogged perseverance, Mahiru crossed the finish line as the words First Place flashed across the screen. She turned to look at Amane, obviously proud of herself.

After a hard-won battle with the racing game, Mahiru had achieved the glory of finishing first.

Though she'd ended up in last place on so many earlier tries, Mahiru had refused to quit and kept going, improving her ranking bit by bit until at last, she won. Such investment had probably made the victory quite emotional.

Mahiru's expression seemed to proclaim "I did it!" and Amane dutifully clapped in admiration.

"That's great. I could tell you really tried hard," he praised.

"Yep!" Perhaps because Mahiru was enjoying the praise, her usual demeanor had softened, and she appeared a little bashful. She didn't break into a huge, obvious grin but instead wore a fleeting, shy curl of the lips that looked ever-so-slightly pleased. It seemed so sweet that it was hard to believe it belonged to the same cool, reserved person.

Recently, Mahiru had been acting more like a regular teenage girl and less like a perfect young lady. Today most of all, she was really acting like a kid. Her cherubic smile had something innocent about it, and looking at her, Amane felt his sense of reason begin to give way as the roaring desire to hold her close rose within him. The urge to pet Mahiru like a cat seized control of his arm, and before he knew it, Amane found himself reaching out toward her.

"Is something the matter?" Mahiru asked.

Quickly, Amane regained control of his wayward limb. "Ah, n-no, it's nothing. You really got good at this, h-huh?"

"I'm getting better?"

"For sure. You're way better than when you first started."

"Thank you. It was a lot of fun, so I guess I got pretty engrossed."
Mahiru chuckled to herself.

Amane avoided making eye contact by crossing the room and
retrieving a small box from a basket on the shelf. "Let's say this is your
prize for first place," he said.

"Ah, um, that's really not—"

"If you don't like the idea of a prize, then think of this as something left behind by a stout old man with a white beard and a red
suit."

It was a Christmas present that Amane had carelessly forgotten to
give Mahiru the day before.

Since Mahiru's birthday and Christmas weren't that far apart,
Amane had expected some difficulty picking out this second gift.
Thankfully, he'd also gotten a little more familiar with the practice,
so it surprisingly wound up not being as tough to choose a Christmas
present as it had been finding one for Mahiru's birthday.

Mahiru blinked rapidly, as if the reference to a Christmas present had just reminded her that today was in fact Christmas, and she
nervously accepted the box. At Amane's urging, she carefully undid
the wrapping.

Well, it's nothing special, though, Amane thought.

She opened the box and slowly took out the gift. It was a leather
key holder.

Expecting Mahiru to feel uncomfortable if Amane got her something too expensive, Amane had avoided getting a fancy brand-name
item. He'd selected this one purely because the design seemed like it
would suit Mahiru.

It was simple, with flowers and ivy carved into the leather, making it perfect for everyday use. Amane wasn't too well versed in flowers, so he didn't know exactly which ones were featured in the design,

but he thought their dainty forms suited Mahiru well, and that's why he'd chosen it.

"Well, I gave you my spare key and all. If you don't want to use it, that's okay, too," Amane said.

"No, I definitely will, thank you. You've got a better sense of style than I expected, Amane," Mahiru replied.

"What do you mean, better than expected?"

"I mean, normally you just wear sweatpants or jeans... It's not like you're into fashion or anything."

"I just don't own anything besides functional clothes."

Getting dressed up in nicer outfits was a tedium that Amane avoided whenever possible. He'd never had the occasion to show Mahiru what he looked like in better clothing, so she'd only ever seen him in his school uniform and casual house clothes. It was no wonder she assumed he had no fashion sense. Such a guess had been right on the money, and Amane didn't seem likely to dispel that slovenly impression anytime soon.

"...If you made an effort, you'd probably look pretty good, you know? You kept up your appearance in middle school, didn't you?" Mahiru asked.

"That was because my mom forced me to... Wait, how do you know that?"

"Shihoko sent me this picture and said, 'Here's what he could look like if he tried'..."

"Unbelievable."

Amane was shocked to see the photo of the time his mother had dressed him up and brought him to work. Silently, Amane cursed his mother's indiscretion.

"...That style didn't suit me."

"I suppose you're right, Amane. You know, you never make eye contact, and your face is always hidden behind your hair, but I think you have rather distinguished features…"

Mahiru's small hand stretched out toward Amane's face, and her white palm brushed against his forehead as she pushed his long bangs upward. She was looking at him with a curious expression. He didn't think his face was anything to marvel over; it was perfectly ordinary—not quite ugly and not quite handsome. Amane began to wonder why Mahiru was staring so intently at him.

"…What is it?" he asked.

"Nothing. Your eyes look livelier than they used to, that's all," Mahiru replied.

Without looking away, Mahiru reminded Amane that several months earlier, his face had been vacant like a zombie's.

While Mahiru continued to stare, Amane was beginning to feel uncomfortable that a girl, not to mention an incredible beauty, was staring at him so intently. He wondered what she found so fascinating about his boring looks.

Eventually, he couldn't stand it anymore. Amane slowly reached out and brushed a lock of hair away from Mahiru's own lovely face. He was hesitant to touch her, but she had reached out and touched his hair so casually that he thought she'd probably forgive him for doing the same. It would only be the faintest moment of contact; surely that much would be all right.

But wow, she really is beautiful…

Mahiru was much prettier than the glamorous models in the magazines that had previously been scattered around Amane's room—and much more appealing. Something about her felt amazing every time he looked upon her.

Photographs, Amane knew, couldn't be trusted anyway. Even if they could capture a moment of beauty, preserving it in time, photographs could be made to deceive. Mahiru, however, was standing there before him in the flesh. Her beauty was real—unadulterated. Amane didn't think he could ever get tired of beholding such a creature.

As Amane continued studying her features, Mahiru's eyes started to shift, and she pulled away from him, dropping her controller. Amane wondered what was bothering her as she hugged a nearby couch cushion tight against her chest.

"Um. So…right. I have a Christmas present for you, too."

"Um, oh, thanks."

Amane was about to ask what on earth it might be, when Mahiru cut him off by pulling out a nicely decorated gift bag from her purse. Hastily, she pushed it into his hands.

"All right, I'm going to prepare dinner."

"Huh? Y-you are…?"

With those words, Mahiru quickly stood and moved to the kitchen. Amane was left with nothing but bewilderment at the overly rapid development.

After Amane finished washing the dishes from dinner, he returned to the living room to find that Mahiru was restless. She was sitting beside him, in the way they had recently grown accustomed to, but this time, Mahiru was having trouble maintaining her composure. She'd been averting her gaze all through dinner, too.

This was a kind of self-consciousness that Mahiru had seemed previously incapable of, prompting Amane to wonder if something had happened. Perhaps it had something to do with her giving him the gift? When Amane had given Mahiru the teddy bear, he, too, had felt like running away, and it'd been difficult for him to calm down. Maybe Mahiru was experiencing a similar sort of anxiety.

"By the way, can I open this?" Amane asked.

"P-please do."

Amane picked up the gift from where he'd left it sitting atop the coffee table, and Mahiru nodded somewhat hesitantly. Concluding that she was indeed nervous about giving him a present, Amane untied the ribbon fastening the bag.

Right away, he could tell from the feel and weight that it was something made out of cloth. When Amane pulled it out and saw it to be a length of black-and-white houndstooth, he wasn't sure what it was. After spreading out the whole object, however, he immediately understood.

"A scarf?"

It appeared to be quite soft and luxurious. Surely, this would keep him warm if he wound it around his neck.

"…Well, you're indifferent to fashion, and you always seem cold on the way to school, so…"

"I can really use it; and wow, it feels so nice."

"Quality is important when you're choosing something that you'll be using every day," Mahiru explained.

As Mahiru was someone who only wore high-quality clothes, Amane was sure she knew what she was talking about. Mahiru seemed like the type who considered it a waste of time to buy cheap things, preferring to use well-made products that would last for a long time, instead. If this scarf met her standards, it had to be very nice indeed.

Amane could tell just by touching it that the scarf had a luxurious texture and was soft enough not to bother even sensitive skin.

Impressed with Mahiru's high standards, Amane waved the gift at her while she watched him with a stiff expression.

"Can I try it on?" Amane asked.

"I gave it to you, so you can do whatever you like," Mahiru answered curtly.

"Roger."

Amane smiled at her blunt response and wrapped the scarf

around himself. He could feel the quality of the fabric even more on his neck, where the skin was more sensitive. It kept all the warmth in without letting too much air pass through. The feel of the fabric was soothing and snug. As Amane was still inside, it was hard to tell just how effective the scarf would be, but he trusted it would undoubtedly keep him comfortable throughout the winter months.

"Wow, it's super warm."

"That's great."

Amane put on a gentle smile, and Mahiru answered with a relieved smile of her own. Recently, Mahiru had begun to show Amane her many kinds of smiles more frequently, and he found himself staring again at her enchanting features.

...When she looks like that, she really does seem like an angel...

Sure, everyone at school said Mahiru looked heavenly, but Amane thought it was far more attractive when she smiled like this and showed her true self.

"Wh-what is it?" Mahiru had noticed that Amane was staring straight at her. Her eyes shifted left and right before fixing themselves back on the one gazing at her.

"Nothing; I was just thinking that you seem much more relaxed compared to when I first met you."

"...Is that so?"

Mahiru looked surprised, and Amane laughed a little.

"Yeah. Before, you were all stuck-up and not cute at all."

"That was terrible of me, not being cute," Mahiru said sarcastically.

"Come on—don't sulk... Now you're way more... How should I put it? I think you just look better. I was thinking that the way you smile now is way cuter. It's really kind of a shame you weren't smiling like that sooner."

Mahiru had always been beautiful, but some quality of that changed in how she carried herself.

The angelic smile that she showed at school had the beauty of something to be appreciated from a distance. It was a fragile thing that was not be touched.

The cold look that she'd first given Amane held the appeal of something wreathed in thorns to keep humans from getting too close.

Now her soft and innocent smile had a welcoming warmth that made Amane want to caress and cherish her.

Amane thought about how Mahiru had changed. She'd slowly gotten used to being around him, and she'd slowly opened up her heart. As he thought back on the time they'd spent together, Amane felt a ticklish sensation gradually rising through his chest and up into his cheeks.

"I'm happy that you can smile so naturally now, and that you've gotten used to hanging around with me, and… What are you doing?"

Amane's sentence was physically cut off as Mahiru lifted the scarf up from around his neck to cover his face with the fabric. She didn't wrap it tight, but it grew a bit stuffy and hot as the material trapped Amane's breath.

"…Please just be quiet for a bit," Mahiru commanded.

"What for?"

"…Nothing."

Amane didn't understand this sudden outburst of eccentric behavior. He grabbed the wrist of her hand that was holding up the scarf and pushed it back down. With his vision restored, he could see Mahiru's flaxen hair and the tinge of color spread across her cheeks, and he noticed that she was trembling slightly. As she looked at him, she grew even more flushed.

He wondered why she was making such an odd face, and then it suddenly hit him that there could be only one answer.

"…Don't tell me…you're embarrassed?"

"Shut up."

Mahiru turned away sharply, which only served to confirm what Amane had said. Without meaning to, Amane smiled as he mused that the angel sure could be prickly about things like this.

Mahiru groaned and quietly muttered, "I'm going outside for some air." Then she quickly made for the veranda.

Through the window, Amane could see it snowing just like it had the day before, but Mahiru didn't seem to care and stepped out onto the balcony anyway.

Chilly air rushed into the apartment, and Amane shivered. Though Mahiru immediately shut the door, a touch of cold still hung about the living room. Amane let out a quiet sigh.

It's fine for her to run away to hide her embarrassment, but she could at least do it in a slightly warmer outfit.

Mahiru had obviously picked her clothes assuming she would be spending the day inside—or at least wearing a heavy jacket if she went out. She'd clearly prioritized looks over warmth, and her slender body was sure to chill quickly in the cold.

Amane cursed under his breath and picked up the blanket that was lying over the back of the sofa.

It's super dangerous to stand outside in the snow wearing such thin clothing.

After pulling on his coat, Amane followed Mahiru out onto the veranda and wrapped the blanket around her shoulders.

"Getting some fresh air is fine, but you'll catch a cold like that," chided Amane.

Mahiru quickly turned to face him. "...Isn't that my line?" Clearly, she'd calmed down, as she'd answered with her usual demeanor and expression, though there was a bit of a sulking tone to her voice. Maybe she was feeling down because Amane had said something that called back to the conversation from when they'd first met.

"Hmph. That only happened because I didn't get in a bath and warm up like I should have. Simple negligence," Amane reminded.

"Next time you get soaked like a drowned rat, make sure you warm yourself up right. If I'm there, I'll be sure to toss you in the bath myself," Mahiru shot back.

"What're you, my mom?"

There were definitely times when Mahiru said some rather motherly things.

With a smile, Amane recalled his first encounter with the angel. It'd been around the time autumn usually started getting cold, about halfway through October. He hadn't expected to come down with a fever just from getting a little wet, but the weather had gotten chillier far faster than it usually did back in his hometown. Thinking back on it, Amane admitted to himself that perhaps he really had been careless.

The most surprising part of the whole situation, however, had definitely been Mahiru nursing him back to health.

"...Y'know, it's already been two months since we started talking...," Amane said wistfully.

"You're right. And to think, your room was so dirty! It was terrible... Now it only haunts my memories," Mahiru quipped.

"Oh, hush. I'm keeping it clean now, right?"

"And who do you owe for that?"

"Why, Lady Mahiru, of course. It makes me want to bow down in humble gratitude."

"You don't need to do that, geez."

Back on that rainy day, Amane would never have believed that he and Mahiru would get to a point where they could banter like this. It all seemed so long ago now, but really, it had only been a short while back. A lot had changed in those two months. Time had really flown by.

A silence fell over the two, and suddenly, everything was quiet.

The snow, which had been starting and stopping in fits since yesterday, was now drifting softly down from the sky, painting the surrounding apartment buildings in a pale hue.

Amane and Mahiru's building was in residential area, plus it was Christmas, so the area was hushed. From some apartment nearby, the pair could very faintly hear the sounds of a Christmas song, though not well enough to decipher any lyrics.

Mahiru exhaled a little white puff, and Amane's ears caught that sound better than any other.

"…It's kind of a strange feeling." Mahiru was the one to break the silence. "At first, I was wondering 'What's up with this guy?'"

"Well, I guess that's not surprising. Anyone would be suspicious if someone suddenly forced an umbrella on them… What do you think now?"

"Hmm, let's see. I'd have to say…you're a whole lot of work." Mahiru turned away after her ambiguous answer.

"You're not wrong." Amane smiled while leaning against the veranda railing. "…You know, I never thought that we would get close enough to be eating meals together like this, either. To be honest, I always thought of you as someone to be admired from a distance. I never considered ever getting involved with you."

"That was certainly honest…though I knew that already. That's precisely why I trust you," Mahiru said, and her body shook with laughter.

Amane knew that Mahiru only accepted him in her life because he wasn't attracted to her; and apparently, she felt the same way.

"Still, I'm glad that I got to know you like this. My life has really improved a ton, I'm happy because I get to eat delicious food every day, and I feel at ease when I'm hanging out with you," Amane declared.

"...You really think so?"

"I do. I'm incredibly grateful for these past two months. Thank you." Amane couldn't have been more sincere if he tried. It was thanks to Mahiru that his standard of living had gone up and that he got to enjoy a delicious meal every day. Surprisingly, Amane had also discovered that he could enjoy talking to a girl without any sort of awkward expectations. It'd even become something he looked forward to. Even better, Mahiru would occasionally flash him adorable reactions when Amane teased her, and he never got tired of those.

Recently, she's started to laugh more, too.

As Amane had realized before, Mahiru had indeed started displaying a richer array of emotions, a change that only made her more endearing. Amane would never actually act on his feelings, of course, but...just looking at her made him feel at peace.

Mahiru's eyes were wide, and Amane couldn't tell whether the slight redness in her cheeks was because of the cold or because she was embarrassed.

"No, thank *you* very much," she said.

"But I didn't do anything." From Amane's perspective, Mahiru was the one who'd done everything for him. He was sure he hadn't given the girl anything in return, but she slowly shook her head in disagreement.

"...I'm grateful for things that you aren't aware of, Amane," Mahiru explained.

"Hmm... Each of us telling the other what we're thankful for has sort of an end-of-the-year vibe. I guess that's not all that weird, since the year is about to end."

Curiously, both Amane and Mahiru had thanked the other for certain things, despite the new year still being six days away.

Mahiru's eyes sparkled at the mention of the end of the year, and she let a little laugh slip out. "Ha-ha, that's right. It's still a little early, but…Happy New Year, Amane. Let's make it a good one."

"…Yeah, Happy New Year." Amane nodded and smiled at Mahiru's heaven-sent proposal.

Then Mahiru suddenly said, "I'm freezing; let's go on inside, shall we?" She turned around and opened the glass door that led back to Amane's living room.

Amane caught a glimpse of her ears, which had turned bright red in the frosty air, and he agreed that it was best to retreat inside so as not to catch cold.

…*One way or another, I guess I've also taken a liking to this lifestyle. That's probably why my chest feels so warm.* As he followed Mahiru back into the apartment, Amane watched the gentle swaying of her soft, flaxen hair and smiled secretly to himself.

He hoped that in the days to come, he would continue to see more of the angel who lived next door.

Afterword

Nice to meet you. My name is Saeki.

I trust you enjoyed *The Angel Next Door*?

I set out to write this book as a heartwarming, slow-but-steady, fluffy little romantic comedy, and I'm pretty sure I managed to do just that.

Both characters started out rather distant and cold, but they gradually came to trust each other and found themselves charmed by the other before they knew what was happening. It was quite enjoyable to write those changes in their emotions and their relationship.

I think it's good to have those kinds of stories where people slowly get to know each other, too. As for what I want to say through my work, well, I think slow and steady is just the best! That's what I have to say.

This work underwent some revisions in the time between it first being published online to when it was made into a book, but honestly, Amane and Mahiru aren't quite focused directly on each other yet. The real fun begins in Volume 2.

I'm still going to take things slow and steady as the series continues, but I plan for them both to take steps toward the other. Both characters having unrequited love is the best!

I gave our heroine Mahiru her nickname of angel, but it was the illustrations that really made her live up to that nickname. My thanks to Hazano Kazutake. You really made Mahiru, aka the school angel, even more charming.

Actually, when I met with the head editor, I happened to put forth the idea that Kazutake would be good for the illustrations. Imagine my surprise when I heard the offer had been accepted!

I was so excited to work with a master whose drawings I'd admired for so long. Thank you so much for taking charge of the illustrations!

You can tell from looking at Kazutake's incredibly charming illustrations, but every character in this book is cute. Reviewing the final drawings was almost too much for me. The angel actually looks heavenly.

I am just brimming with gratitude for your incredible work!

Well then, we've come to the end, but I still need to express my gratitude to everyone who's helped me along the way.

To the lead editor, who put so much effort into getting this book published, to everyone in the GA Books editorial section, to everyone in the sales department, to the proofreaders, to Hazano Kazutake, to everyone at the printing office, and to all of you who've picked up this book, I extend my humblest gratitude.

As I lay down my pen, it is my sincerest wish that we will all meet again in the next volume.

Thank you so much for reading all the way to the end!

The Angel Next Door Spoils Me Rotten

Special Bonus Short Story

A Power Outage, Anxiety, and Warmth

"Ah!"

Amane let out a panicked yelp as he was suddenly plunged into darkness.

The weather had been calling for storms all week due to an unusual pressure front, and indeed, the sounds of thunder and heavy rain outside were unceasing. But Amane hadn't expected it to get bad enough to knock out the power.

After an especially loud crack of thunder, the lights went out all at once, from the bulbs to the television. It was a total blackout.

Luckily, his computer had been unplugged, so it likely hadn't suffered any damage, but he would have to check the other appliances later.

"Do you have your phone? I left mine in a backpack in my bedroom."

He wished he had a flashlight handy, but a phone would have to do. Unfortunately, Amane had left his in his room, but he figured Mahiru would have hers. She had been sitting next to him, working on problems in a textbook, when the lights cut out.

However, there was no reply.

"...Mahiru?" he called out anxiously.

Amane thought he felt something tugging on his sleeve. He asked what happened, and still, there was no answer. He blindly extended a hand toward where Mahiru had been sitting, and brushed up against something slender that he assumed was Mahiru's arm... It was easy to tell that she was trembling as she started and pulled away.

There was a loud *thud* as something fell down, and then a groan. He heard a grumbling voice come from the floor.

"What a disgrace..."

"...Um, sorry I startled you."

"...No. I startled myself; that's all."

Mahiru didn't seem particularly bothered by her fall from the sofa as she groped around and found her original position.

Amane was worried that she had landed hard on something, but she didn't seem to be in pain or anything. Then, perhaps while Mahiru searched for the hem of Amane's shirt again, her fingertips brushed against him lightly.

It tickled, and without thinking, he grabbed her slim wrist, and she started trembling again. This time, she didn't fall off the sofa.

"Looking for something?"

"...Are you being sarcastic?"

"Why in the world would I be?"

"I thought you would make fun of me for getting so shaken up by a little blackout..."

"I'm not that much of an ass."

Usually, Mahiru was very levelheaded and not the kind to scare easily—but she was still a teenager, and even an adult could feel anxious if the power suddenly went out.

Outside, the thunder rolled on, accompanying the endless drumming of raindrops, but inside the apartment, it was quiet and still. Mahiru continued fiddling nervously with the hem of Amane's shirt, but she didn't make any moves to brush off his hand. He had been a little nervous about touching her at first, but now he gently squeezed her hand.

"...So I guess you're not a big fan of the dark?"

He spoke to her softly and could more or less make out that she shook her head.

"...I don't hate it, but..."

"Mm-hmm?"

"...I just don't like it when it's bright one moment and dark the next—that's all."

"Ah, okay."

"I'm not really afraid of the dark, and I don't feel scared."

"Sure, yeah."

Mahiru stubbornly dismissed her fears in an even more aloof tone than usual, but Amane had spent enough time with her to know it was all an adorable bluff.

He smiled slightly, thinking that the cover of darkness could be a good thing, but Mahiru added in a small voice, "...There's just one thing."

He stopped smiling and leaned slightly toward Mahiru. "Hmm?"

"...When we sit like this, I know I'm not alone, and I feel better," Mahiru mumbled. She sounded relieved.

"I see," said Amane, and he gently squeezed her hand again.

"...The power's back on. I'm going to check my appliances."

The moment the lights in the room flashed to life, Mahiru gently slipped out of Amane's hold and stood up.

Amane smiled wryly at her transparent change in attitude, but he noticed that the ears poking out from under her flaxen hair were red and decided to not say anything.

He stood up, too, to go look at the circuit breaker and check that nothing had malfunctioned. When he passed Mahiru, he heard a small "Thank you" and couldn't help but stare at her.

In a fluster, Mahiru turned away quickly and went to the kitchen to escape. Amane simply scratched his cheek and headed for the washroom to check on the breakers there.

Once inside, he noticed that his reflection in the mirror had slightly flushed cheeks. "That's weird," he muttered as he turned away bashfully.